A TOWN CALLED

Vengeance

D0369290

MAY 09 2018

A TOWN CALLED Vengeance

K E V I N   W O L F

North Star
—EDITIONS—
Mendota Heights, Minnesota

First Edition
First Printing, 2018

Book design by Sarah Taplin
Cover design by Jake Slavik
Cover images by Pgiam/iStockphoto, trekandshoot/iStockphoto, Mircea Costina/Shutterstock, kordi_vahle/Pixabay, Joxerra/Pixabay

Library of Congress Cataloging-in-Publication Data (pending)
978-1-63583-906-7

North Star Editions, Inc.
2297 Waters Drive
Mendota Heights, MN 55120
www.northstareditions.com

Printed in the United States of America

For Katie and Karrie
My daughters

Chapter One

If I thought prayers were answered, I would have asked for relief from the desert's heat. But if the good Lord might hear only one of this sinner's requests, I'd save that prayer. A time could come when my wits and the silver bullet in my vest pocket might not be enough. And it's always best to hedge your bets.

The stagecoach lurched over the rutted trail-road. June's head bounced against my shoulder. Sweat beaded on her face and the dust turned her corn-silk hair gray.

Her eyes opened with the next jolt, and she yawned. "Kepler, if I'd've counted every bump 'tween here and Brokeheart, I'da run out of numbers by now."

I touched her face. "You heard the driver. He intends to roll all night. We'll be in Vengeance by sunup tomorrow."

June wiped the dampness from her face with her shirt-sleeve and a smile emerged. "You gonna buy me that new dress like you promised?"

"I am." I tried to act stern.

Her eyes widened. "Bath, too?"

"With hot water and soap." My sternness lost, I smiled back.

"New home for the both of us," she said. "All that bad in Colorado so far behind us now. You're gonna be a respectable newspaper reporter. No more playin' poker in some dark old saloon."

"Last night's winnings are paying for that dress and bath." I caught the very end of her hair in my fingers and stroked its softness. "And respect is something one has to earn."

The splash of freckles on her nose wrinkled. "Think I'll ever earn it, Kepler?"

"I told you, no more talk like that. No one in Vengeance knows anything about Colorado. It's like you're brand new." With each mile closer, I weighed my own reasons for coming to the Arizona territory. The silver bullet in my vest pocket and a newspaper story tucked in my coat meant everything would not be brand-new for me.

June sat up. "Driver's stoppin' the stage. Ain't time to water the horses, is it?"

I pushed my head out of the window as the wagon jerked to a halt. The driver wrapped the reins around the brake handle, pulled his Winchester from its scabbard, and dropped to the ground.

"What is it, Ford?" I stepped onto the roadway beside him.

"That she-wolf"—he jacked a shell into his rifle's chamber—"it's been runnin' that ridge just ahead of us for the last two hours. Makes my skin crawl."

Sweat dripped from my face, but my insides turned icy cold.

"Look at it just starin' at us." Ford knelt and raised the gun to his cheek. "I'm gonna fry its bacon for sure."

At the edge of a fringe of sage, a long rifle shot away, the wolf sat on its haunches. Its eyes seemed fixed on us. Not just us, but me.

A black soldier on a black gelding rode up to the stagecoach. "Can't be stoppin' here."

"I didn't ask for your help and don't take orders from no nigra sergeant," Ford said, clamping his face tighter to the rifle. "That devil wolf been followin' us for six miles."

The five other Buffalo Soldiers brought their horses to a stop. Their sergeant motioned for them to stay mounted.

The driver's rifle cracked. Dirt jumped a yard in front of the wolf. All sounds stopped, and the desert went ghostly quiet. The wolf tipped its nose to the sky. At its howl, a cloud passed over the sun. Shadows stretched over the desert around us like inky blots. The stage's team of horses skittered in their harness.

"Damn," Ford hissed, working another round into his rifle.

Before he could fire, a gunshot shattered the stillness. The team's lead horse screamed in pain. The animal reared and fought its harness as blood spurted from a ragged hole in its ribs. The horse's feet gave way and it fell to the ground still tangled in its traces.

"Apaches!" the sergeant screamed to his men.

Another shot. Wood splintered from the stagecoach. I pushed June back from the doorway. "Stay down."

Ford lunged up from the ground. The toe of one boot found the wheel's rim and he was onto the driver's seat. He hauled back on the reins, holding the terrified horses. "Cut that dead horse free. We gotta run for it."

The sergeant pulled a knife from his belt and dove to the front of the team. I caught hold of the bridle of the lead horse and pulled it away from its dead harness mate. Dirt catapulted into the air as an Apache's bullet struck the ground just inches from my foot.

Four troopers jerked carbines from their saddles and took positions at the road's edge, guns at their shoulders.

Smoke rose from the gun barrels as they snapped shots at the hillside. The fifth soldier led the frightened horses away from the fight.

The sergeant slashed down with his knife, hacking through the leather straps. He stretched over the dead horse and cut away more of the harness. "It's free. Go. Go." He pushed up to his feet.

An Apache's rifle bellowed. The bullet slapped the sergeant's leg. Bone cracked. His eyes rolled back in their sockets.

I caught him around the shoulders as he fell, dragged him to the stagecoach, and lifted him up and inside. The stage pitched forward. I caught the window frame and fought to keep my feet under me. Over my shoulder, puffs of gun smoke from the Apache's rifles showed on the hillside. The wolf sat rooted to the same place. It tilted its head in a deep howl as the stage raced away, and then after a moment the wolf bounded after us.

The demon from Colorado had found me in this desert.

June's dress front shined slick with blood. She ripped a ruffle from her petticoat and clamped it over the gory wound on the sergeant's leg. He thrashed with each bounce of the stage, but the man never cried out.

I swung inside the swaying coach and slammed the door shut. Ford cursed at the team and the ends of his reins popped in the air.

At the next curve in the road, the stage leaned as if only two wheels still touched on the ground. June slid across the seat. As her grip on the sergeant's leg loosened, blood fountained up between her fingers. The wheels crashed back to earth. My head cracked the roof. A bullet whined through the air. Slivers exploded from the place on the seat where June had been only seconds before.

I wrapped my arms around June's waist and pulled her to me. Gravity won out and we tumbled. Shadows took away the light. Stones, dirt, and torn pieces of brush filled the air around my face. Motion blurred time.

"Get 'em out!" a voice cried.

Black hands pulled June from me. I raised my arms toward the voices. Someone caught hold and hauled me up into the sunlight.

"Sergeant Pope?" another voice asked.

"He's hurt. Bad," I answered.

My back rested against the crippled coach's floor. Above my head, a wheel still spun on its axle. Though some shadow filled my brain, I called, "June?"

"Here, Kep." She scrambled to me.

"You all right?"

"I think so."

"What—"

A young buffalo soldier hovered close to us. "Apaches killed another horse. Driver, he couldn't do nothin'. Coach turned over."

A wolf howled.

The soldier lifted his head. "Listen."

Another wolf answered. Then another.

"Like that wolf is tellin' the Apaches where we are," the soldier whispered. "God in heaven help us."

"Soldier!" It was Pope. The sergeant lifted himself on his elbows. Blood stained his sun-bleached trousers. "Report," he barked through his teeth.

The trooper bit into the back of his hand and peered at

Pope. "Stage team run off. Wagon all broke up. Driver, he jumped free." The trooper hung his head. "When we stop for the wagon, Hooks, he take the horses. Apaches killed him. Got our horses, too."

Pope bit down on his lip. "Ground?"

"We down in a gulley. No deeper than a man's knees. Not much cover, though. We stay close to the stagecoach."

"No. Form up your skirmish line out there." Pope jerked his head toward the hill the Apaches had fired from. "Face 'em down." He slumped onto his back. "We need to look as powerful mean as we can. We could be here a long time."

———————

Desert dust etched every wrinkle in the black cavalryman's face beside me. "Dead men smell worse than dead horses," he said.

The dead horse lay on the road. The trooper's body was somewhere in the sage. The breeze that brought the hint of evening now carried the stench of death.

The trooper's dark eyes studied the sand and twisted cactus. "Hope that sun goes down soon. This heat like the edge of a straight razor."

Still air sliced open, and a dirt clod bigger than my fist jumped into the air ten feet in front of where I lay. Then the noise of a gunshot rolled toward our hiding place on the gully bank. Another bullet flew over our heads, and dirt leaped as many feet behind us. The sound of the Indian's rifle followed.

"Land o' Goshen. They'll lay out there and lob bullets at us 'til we try to run for it." The buffalo soldier flattened the side of his head onto the arroyo bank. "Keep down," he snapped at the three troopers spread out along the bank. He twisted his neck so I could see his face. "Boxin' us for range like U.S. Grant's own artillery. If those Apaches are spottin' their shots, next ones'll be right on top of us."

Swack. Then *bang.*

"Hit the stagecoach." His face eased up from the dirt. "Maybe they don't know just where—" *Zing.*

His head burst like a ripe melon. Shattered bone, blood, and bits of brain splattered my face. In the next second, I wrenched the Springfield from the dead soldier's hands and swung it up over the edge of the gulley. Through the smear of his blood in my eyes I squinted down the sights. A puff of white gun smoke hung on the distant hillside.

"Get down, Kepler," Sergeant Pope screamed from behind the overturned stagecoach.

Anger replaced reason. I aimed the carbine at the top of the smoke cloud and jerked the trigger. The recoil slapped the rifle into my shoulder, and I ducked down onto the bloodstained sand sure that I had wasted a bullet that we might need later.

"You men." Pope's voice fought his pain. "Fire on that hill. Make 'em keep their heads down, hear me?"

The troopers slithered up to the rim of the embankment. Three carbine shots smashed the hot air.

Smoke showed on the hill and a bullet whizzed overhead. A soldier's carbine barked. The blast of the trooper's rifle met the incoming sound of the Apache's shot and rumbled like thunder.

Then all went still.

Seconds stretched into minutes. Each greasewood branch that shimmered in the afternoon heat became a warrior with a stolen rifle. But no more gunshots came.

One of the troopers crept along the sandy wash to the dead soldier beside me. Ants the color of dried blood swarmed over the ruined face. One ant, carrying a tiny fragment of white bone, crossed the back of my hand. My stomach went sick and I flicked the insect away.

The trooper covered the dead man's head with a scrap of saddle blanket. Only the old man's wooly white hair showed. Lines of ants disappeared under the blanket's edges.

"Suh," the soldier whispered. "I'm gonna split up his ammo 'tween the rest of us." He pulled the cartridge box from the dead man's belt. "Still has water in his canteen. Reckon Sergeant Pope and the others might be needin' some." He pushed the canvas-covered tin into my hand. "Hang on to that carbine."

"What's your name, boy?"

"Private Freeman Taylor, suh." Sweat glistened off skin as black as coal.

"How old are you?"

"Seventeen." He was the same age as June, but eyes older than the desert stared back at me.

"What was his name?" I nodded at the body between us.

"Everybody just call him Moses. On account he was so old." The trooper's tongue touched his lips. "He was a good soldier."

"I'm sure he was. I'll take the water to Pope."

"Suh." Taylor slipped the Colt revolver from the holster under Moses's body. "You might want to give this to your lady."

He pressed the gun into my hand. "Tell her to save the last bullet." He turned to look at the hillside where the shots had come from. "I done seen what bad things Apaches do to white women."

My stomach squeezed tight and moved up my throat. I tucked the long-barreled pistol into my belt and nodded. June peered from the corner of the stagecoach. I wanted to pray that she hadn't heard the trooper. Too much in my past made me sure God wouldn't hear my prayers.

"Top sergeant done got us outta tighter spots then this 'un." Taylor slid the barrel of his Springfield over the gully's rim. "When you ready, go fast. We cover you."

I slipped the canteen inside my shirtfront and slipped into the tinder-dry bunchgrass in the arroyo bottom. Grass stalks shattered into hundreds of sharp needles, piercing my pants and stabbing my palms. I lay for an instant, waiting for an Apache's bullet to tear into me, then pushed up and scrambled for the cover of the wagon.

June caught me in her arms and pulled me tight. Red veins webbed her eyes. I touched my lips to her forehead. "We'll get out of this." I wanted those words to comfort her, though I feared they might be lies.

Sergeant Pope's ramrod-straight back propped against the stagecoach bottom; his head found a spot of shade from one of the wheels. "Who got kilt?" The words wheezed out.

"Moses."

"Lord in Heaven." His shoulders dropped. "First Hooks, then Moses. Never lost a man on my patrols 'til now." Pope's hand clutched at his thigh.

"How's the leg?"

"Miss June bandaged it up and stopped the bleedin'. Think the bullet broke the bone." In spite of the pain I saw in his face, his words came out flat and even.

"I brought water." I held out Moses's bloodstained canteen.

"Miss June first."

June looked at the stains, swallowed hard, and then lifted the canteen to her lips. When she finished, she crawled next to Pope and held the water to his lips. The knot of his Adam's apple slid up and down behind his leathery skin. "Thank you, Miss."

Boot soles scraped sand, and the coach driver dived in behind the overturned wagon. He pressed his back against the wagon's floor next to me. Ford had tied a kerchief over his head to protect his bald skin from the sun. His lost hat lay in the dry grass a dozen steps from where we hid, but in plain view of the Apaches on the bluff.

"It's near flat as a pancake out there." Tobacco juice dribbled from his chin. "No way they can get around behind us without our knowin' it." He jerked a Bowie knife from his belt and stabbed it into the dirt. "Somethin' ain't right. They got the horses." He jabbed the knife point in again. "No more than five or six of 'em thieving bucks. Why risk goin' up against our rifles?"

Ford wiped a grimy hand across his forehead. "Know somethin' else? That same she-wolf's a-settin' out there in the cactus just watchin' the whole thing. Like she's gonna waltz in here and eat the flesh from our bones when the Apaches are done with us."

June's fingers dug into my arm and she sucked in a breath.

"Sorry, ma'am." Ford sunk his knife hilt-deep in the dirt.

"Where's the wolf?" I scanned the harsh landscape.

Ford pointed to where the arroyo opened onto the

desert floor. "Just outta rifle range, or I woulda shot her myself."

My fingers searched my vest pocket. The cool touch of the silver bullet I always carried brought but a bit of relief. Would one bullet be enough?

"It'll be dark soon." Ford looked at Pope. "Apaches don't fight at night, ain't that right?"

"Most likely these young bucks will tire out and want to get back to their women." Pope grimaced. "They'll show off the string of horses they stole and tell stories of how brave they be. We'll sit tight 'til dawn. They be gone then."

Pope waited for Ford to turn away. His glassy eyes found me and he shook his head.

Chapter Two

The orange sun touched the west horizon, scorching away the light until the sky turned the color of ashes. Shadows stretched and filled the arroyo. Our little band huddled around the crippled stagecoach hoping that morning would bring reprieve.

Pope's face was as gray as the sky over us, yet the soldier clung to a stern sense of duty to his men. He ordered his troopers to divide the sentry duty. One man watched the arroyo rim, another the flat ground behind us, while two rested. Lookouts changed every three hours.

Ford snapped the lever of his Winchester open and slammed it shut. "Listen to me," he pushed the words through his clenched teeth. "I say we slip down this draw 'fore the moon's up. There's enough weeds and brush to hide us. We find a place out there in the desert and hole up 'til mornin'. If he's right," Ford nodded at Pope, "and the Apaches are gone, we'll be that much closer to Vengeance. If'n he's wrong and those savages come in for the kill, we'll be gone."

"We can't move Pope. His leg's broken."

"Leave 'im and his nigras. They're paid to fight Apaches."

His stale breath washed over my face. "C'mon, Kepler, you and your woman, let's make a break for it. The three of us got more chance out there then we got here."

June helped Pope take a few drops of water from the

canteen. After he'd drunk, she wiped her finger around the rim and touched a single drop to her lips.

"See there, we ain't got the water to make it through another day of this." Ford gripped his rifle tighter. "You want to watch that woman roast in this heat 'til some Apache dashes in to slit her throat? Or worse?"

Before I could speak, one of Pope's troopers scrambled back to the wagon. "Top Sergeant?" It was Taylor. "I could hear somethin' movin' out there. Not like moccasins—I know you don't want to hear it—but it's those wolves."

"Hush what you say, soldier." Pope's face twisted in pain.

Taylor hung his head. "Yes, sergeant. Heard 'em out there at the top of the arroyo."

I pulled myself up and peered over the coach's broken wheels. A wolf lifted its head and bayed at the rising moon, its sleek body silhouetted against the cobalt sky. Another answered its call. Then another.

Some devil heard their cries and the wind gusted, pelting the back of my head with sand and grit. Stalks of the dry grass that filled the gulley bowed to the hot breath of air and the wolves' howls.

"There," Ford cried out.

From the knoll where the wolves howled, a fiery ball arched into the sky. It hung for an instant and then sped toward the earth behind us.

"Flamin' arrow," Ford cursed.

Fear sliced through me. Someone was coming for us. But who would it be? Apaches with rifles? Or wolves? If God would hear my prayer, I chose Apaches.

Flickers of fire spread in the weeds and brush along the gulley floor. In a gust of wind, the tinder-dry grass burst into flames. Pushed by the demon's wind, a wall of fire swept up the gully toward the stagecoach.

"No-o-o-o," Ford screamed. He fired wildly, first at the wolves on the hillside, then at the curtain of flames. His eyes peeled wide. "I ain't gonna burn," he bellowed.

Blinded by his own madness, Ford struggled to his feet and dodged around the end the wagon. White streaks blazed from the muzzle of his rifle as he fired into the dark before him. He turned and ran from the speeding wall of fire.

Every blade of grass became fuel for the racing inferno. Flames higher than a horse's head licked the night sky and roared like the devil's own choir.

I snatched a canteen from the ground and dumped it on June's hair. "Taylor, wet down Pope." The young soldier's mouth dropped open, and then he scooped up a canteen and spilled it on his sergeant. The other troopers ran to the wagon.

Ash fell on us. Hot air scorched my lungs. The fire raced toward us, crackling as it devoured every weed and bush in its way.

Above the sounds of this hell, Ford shrieked. Snarls and yips from the frenzied pack of wolves filled my ears. Above the sounds of chaos, I heard a man being torn to pieces.

"Grab Pope!" I screamed over the roar of the coming firestorm. "Drag him."

Taylor and another trooper took Pope by the arms. Pope's mouth opened, but the fire's roar stole away the sound of his scream.

I grabbed June's hand. The fire burned nearer. "Trust me," I yelled with my nose touching hers. "Run for all your worth."

Wind whipped the hungry flames closer. I jerked June's hand and screamed to the black soldiers, "Follow me!"

And we hurled ourselves into the hellfire.

My gamble paid off. Driven by the wind, consuming everything in its way, the inferno came at us as a wall of flames. Behind it, only scorched, smoking dirt remained.

June stumbled to her knees as we burst through the blaze. Just below her ear, tiny flames curled the ends of her hair. I smothered them with my bare hands and whirled to see if the soldiers had followed us.

Backlit by the blaze, the four troopers huddled around their sergeant. Pope writhed on the blackened sand. I pushed June into a crevice in the arroyo's bank. "Stay still. The Indians can see us in the firelight. I'll be back."

She tangled her fingers in my shirtsleeve. "D-don't—"

I tugged the pistol Taylor had given me from my belt and pressed it into June's hands. "Take this. If the Apaches—" I couldn't say the words.

"I heard what that soldier said." She wiped her face with her sooty fingers. "Help those men, Kep."

Pope's teeth clenched tight and he clawed at the burnt sand. White-rimmed eyes from four faces stared at me.

"Drag him to the bank." I jerked my head toward where June hid. "Hide him there."

Taylor called over the sound of the fire, "We can't move 'im no more. It'll kill 'im."

Pope raised himself with his elbows. Blood showed glossy black through the bandages on his leg. He fumbled with his belt buckle, unclasped it and pulled his belt free. "Do what he say." The sergeant clamped the leather between his teeth and nodded his head.

Taylor hooked his hands under Pope's arms. Two other troopers took their sergeant by his waist, and the three slid Pope through the dirt to the edge of the gulley. Pope flung his head from side to side with each inch they moved, but no sound came from the man.

The wall of fire danced up the gulch, burning every blade of grass and bush in its way. Where the gulley opened onto the desert, the fire ran out of fuel and played out. Yellow flames flickered on the charred stagecoach where we would have surely burned.

Outlined by the moon, a wolf sat on its haunches and watched from a low hill. From the shadows of the cactus and cholla around it, two more of the animals stalked close to the first. As one, the beastly trio raised their eerie voices. The wind stopped, and the desert became as still as a grave.

As its companions slunk away, the first wolf charged toward me. It stopped in the faint light of the burning stagecoach not thirty yards away. As if reflecting a speck of color from the farthest night star, the slightest glimmer of purple light glowed in its eyes.

I fumbled into my vest pocket for the silver bullet and pulled my mother's revolver from my belt. My hands snapped open the gun, and shaking fingers fought to replace one of the cartridges with the silver one. I slammed the gun barrel in place and raised the weapon. But the she-wolf had melted into the night. As she had taunted me before.

Combing the darkness for any signs of movement, I backed my way to the edge of the arroyo where June and the troopers hid. Pope sprawled on the ground at the bottom of the gulley bank.

June knelt close to the sergeant and brushed the ashes from his face. She turned when she heard me. "He's passed out."

"It's probably best." I looked at the soldiers gathered around their leader. "Let him rest. Nothing we can do now until morning."

"We can pray, suh." Taylor bowed his head.

They trusted their God. I trusted the bullet in my gun.

The three others shut their eyes and joined the boy. June tilted her face forward until her forehead touched the fingers of her folded hands. Taylor's first words were thanks to the Creator for the protection He had offered. Then the young soldier pleaded to spare his sergeant.

While the group prayed, I checked to be sure the silver bullet was under the hammer of my revolver, and then watched the desert night for demons in the form of wolves. If their God wouldn't watch over us, I had to.

Taylor's face came up from his prayer. He made quick gestures with his hands and then pointed to the gulley rim and to a charred stand of paloverdes across from where we hid. The three other troopers split up and dashed through the darkness to the places Taylor's hand had pointed.

"They keep watch, suh." He stared down at his sergeant. "He gonna need water when he come to."

"I know, but—"

"Top Sergeant done taught us a trick for gettin' water out here in this desert." Taylor pulled a jackknife from a pocket of his ash-streaked pants. "Suh, I gonna belly out to some of those big cactus. If'n you cut the top off and scoop out the pulp after awhiles that hole fill up with watery juice. It tastes bad, but it's wet."

Taylor peeked over the rim. "You take my carbine and watch out for me." Taylor looked down at Pope again. "After I cut the cactus, I gonna see if I can sneak out to that dead horse. Might be some hardtack in the saddlebags. Ammo, too." With that, he hoisted himself out of the gulley bottom and crawled out into the desert.

I touched June's head and rubbed my fingers through her dirty corn-silk hair. She moved close to Pope. His chest rose and fell in shallow breaths. June took the old soldier's hand in hers and began to hum. The melody of her favorite hymn carried only a few feet and wisped away into the hot desert night.

False dawn had turned the dark shadows gray, when Taylor slipped back into the gulch. He had the dusty saddlebags and a battered canteen with him. "Canteen's 'bout half full. God watchin' over us, He is. Found some food in these bags, too. We save the good water for Top Sergeant. We get some for ourselves from the cactus I cut." He raised one hand to his mouth, bit down on a cactus spine stuck in the meaty part of his palm, and tugged it out with his teeth.

"Taylor? What about"—I chose the word for the question—"Apaches?"

"No sign at all. Like they disappeared. But—" He looked down at Pope. "There's wolf tracks not ten yards from here."

I touched the pistol in my belt. One silver bullet would not be enough.

"He's burning up with fever," June told me. She raised her arm to shield her eyes from the noontime sun. Pope thrashed about on the sand, and his eyes peeled wide open. One hand grabbed for her wrist.

Taylor scrambled from where he had been dozing against the dirt bank. He pried Pope's hand from June's arm and pinned the sergeant's shoulders down.

Pope moaned at first and then screamed as his eyes fought to focus. "My le-e-e-g."

Taylor tipped the canteen to Pope's mouth. Water spilled from his lips at first. Then the old soldier gulped down a mouthful. A cough rattled up from deep in his chest.

"Top Sergeant, rest yourself." Taylor pulled the water away.

"My leg's burnin' up." Pope clamped his hands on his wounded thigh and struggled to sit.

Taylor pushed him down. "Easy there."

Pope stared up. He swallowed hard. His eyes searched around him. "Apaches?"

"Gone for now," Taylor answered.

"Da men?"

"Got 'em out on sentry like you'd've done."

Pope squirmed and clawed at the bandages on his leg. "Cut the wrap away and tell me how bad."

Taylor's mouth fell open and the boy, not the trooper, looked at me.

"Give me your knife." I held out my hand.

Taylor handed me the knife he had used to cut the cactus.

"Sergeant, I'm going to have Taylor hold you down while I cut away the bandages. I don't want you to move, or I might hurt you more."

As gently as I could, I slipped the point of the blade under the blood-stiff strips of cloth. Pope's leg tensed and he cried out. I tore away the bandages and exposed the bullet-torn flesh just above his knee.

Jagged pieces of ivory-colored bone stuck out from the hole the Apache's bullet had made. Dirt and ash had found their way into the wound. Raw flesh seeped blood, and deep red marks streaked beneath his skin. June turned away and covered her mouth. Waves of sickness inched up my throat.

"How bad is it?" Pope croaked.

I stared down at the gore. It seemed that only scraps of skin and some sliver of bone held the lower leg to his thigh. Infection would set in by morning if it hadn't already. "It's not good."

Pope heaved himself onto his elbows. Sweat beaded on his forehead. "Cut . . . it . . . off, Kepler."

Chapter Three

Taylor sent two troopers to scavenge the remains of the stage for anything we could make use of. They came back with bits of harness, a piece of canvas, and June's carpetbag. The outside of her bag had scorched through. What clothes remained were black and singed.

Taylor filled every canteen we had with the watery juice from the cactus. The last soldier climbed up to the gulley's bank. With his carbine at the ready, the trooper watched the folds in the desert floor for any sign of the Apaches. Taylor was right—the war party had vanished.

June tore the clothes from her bag into strips for bandages. I built a small fire and cleansed the blade of Taylor's jackknife in the blue flames.

"You ever done anything like this before?" Taylor squatted on his heels next to the little fire.

I shook my head. "It's his only hope." I lifted the blade from the fire and stared at the red glowing steel. "Get him to drink as much water as you can pour into him. We'll use his belt as a tourniquet. I want the three of you to hold him down." Beyond that I had only guesses on what I would do.

"Top Sergeant's a good man. God'll love him through this." Taylor reached out and wrapped his fingers around my wrist. "God'll love you, too, Kepler, for doing this. You're a mighty brave man."

I wanted to say, "No I'm not." Instead I told him to call in his troopers.

Taylor split Pope's pant leg to the old man's waist. He looped the belt around the leg just below the hip and drew it tight. With the barrel of his pistol, Taylor twisted the leather tourniquet another full turn. Color drained from the sergeant's blood-starved leg until the skin was as white as the palms of my hands. Pope never looked at me. He spread his arms out across the dirt like the wounded figure on a crucifix.

Taylor signaled for his men. One grabbed Pope's outstretched arm, clamped it to his chest and lay with his whole weight on it. The next copied the first. Taylor stretched out over his sergeant's body with his legs pinning Pope's shoulders to the sand. The weight of his body rested on Pope's good leg. The boy's face was only inches from the gruesome wound.

June knelt by Pope's head. She lifted it so he could take a sip of water and then stuffed a ball of rags into his mouth. She looked at me. Her eyes pleaded for all this to be over.

"Do it, suh." Then Taylor's lips moved in a prayer.

The knife blade touched flesh. A crimson mist spread tiny droplets across Taylor's clamped eyelids. I curled my lip over my teeth and bit down. Drops of Pope's blood made red knots in the dust. I sawed through skin, sinew, and gristle. Whether it was seconds or minutes I couldn't tell. With a last tug of the blade, Pope's severed leg fell heavy into my hands. I tossed the lifeless piece I had cut from his body over the gully's rim and buried my face in my blood-slick hands, certain I had killed the man.

In the next instant, June was beside me, wrapping bandages around the Pope's stump. The sergeant's glassy eyes stared unknowingly at the sky. The veins in his neck thumped with every heartbeat. Each beat seemed slower than the one before.

June wiped my hands and face with the hem of her dress. "I never thought a man could scream like he did—even with those rags in his mouth."

I hadn't heard a sound.

"The fever's burned through him." June touched Pope's face with the tips of her fingers. "Breathin' easy now. Not fightin' for each breath, Kep."

Pope's head rested in Taylor's lap. New tears cut paths through the mix of soot and dirt on the boy's face. "Lord be praised."

I scrambled to Pope and put my fingers on his throat. His pulse felt steady, but weak. "We need to get him to a doctor. How far is it to Vengeance?"

"Walkin' take us two days." Taylor picked a piece of dirt from the old man's face. "Longer if we gotta carry him."

"Have your men rig up some sort of litter. Use the canvas and harness they took from the stage. We'll leave as soon as the sun goes down and travel all night. We can rest in the heat of the day."

"It could kill him." Taylor smeared the dampness on his cheeks.

"No other choice."

Taylor eased Pope's limp body onto the canvas his troopers had lashed between a framework of scorched wood they had taken from the remains of the burnt wagon. The boy slipped his shoulders into a loop of harness strapped to the travois.

"We take our turns pullin' him along. He'd do the same if'n it was one of us."

"I'm sure he would," I told Taylor. "You think a lot of the sergeant, don't you?"

"Never had no father, but him."

I'd never known my father and wondered if I'd ever have someone who would care for me as Taylor cared for his sergeant.

Taylor leaned forward. The leather strap tightened across his chest and the litter skidded over the sandy soil. Orange sunbeams colored the edges of a high skiff of clouds. The heat off the sand eased a bit. I tucked the dead trooper's pistol into my belt, rested a borrowed carbine on my shoulder, and took June's hand in mine.

We followed Taylor down the arroyo. The two troopers fell in behind us. Only the crunch of our footsteps, the scrape of the wood over the sand, and Pope's breathing filled the evening.

A gunshot exploded behind me. When I turned, one of the soldiers had his rifle at his shoulder. The gray wolf darted through the cactus near where we had camped. Dust jumped as his next shot struck near the running animal. The wolf's head hung low, pulling something along the ground.

The trooper lowered his rifle and shoved another cartridge into the chamber. "Damn wolf," he shouted. "It's draggin' off the sergeant's leg."

Chapter Four

Across the valley, at the base of the mountains, Vengeance sat on a smudge of green in the grays and tans of the parched desert. Green promised water. Water would save our lives. But Vengeance was a day's walk from us. Maybe more, dragging Pope.

"Can't stop now. I can see the town." Taylor picked up the strap to Pope's travois and pulled it across his shoulder. "One of you men, help me."

"No, Taylor, you'll kill yourself in this heat. We move at night and rest during the day, no matter how close that town seems." I grabbed the leather harness from his hands. "You'll kill Pope for sure. Find some shade. We rest here until evening."

He tugged back on the leather. "Sergeant's liable not to make it through the heat of another day." One hand dropped to the holster on his hip.

June knelt beside Pope and wiped a scrap of damp rag over his lips. She sat back on her heels and shooed a shiny green fly that hovered near the old man's mouth. The sergeant's eyes made puckered slits on his leathery face.

Taylor's fingers curled around his Colt. He turned to the other troopers sprawled on the ground.

"One of you, get up now." Taylor's eyes went wild and he lifted his pistol from the holster. "We goin' on."

I dipped my right shoulder and made a quarter turn

away from Taylor. Then I pivoted back, throwing all my weight forward, slamming my fist into the boy's jaw.

His pistol skidded across the sand and I fell on top of him, pinning him to the dirt next to Pope's litter. "Taylor, listen to me." My face was not an inch from his. "We're gonna wait 'til dark." The tightness left his muscles. "All we can do now is rest."

Pope's hands clawed at the litter's frayed canvas. He tried to lift his head, but it fell back. "Taylor, you do what he say." The words scratched up from deep inside him. "That's an order." His eyes shut and his head lolled onto his shoulder.

Taylor huffed for his next breath. "Yes, sergeant," he nearly wept.

"You can save him, Taylor, but you got to keep your wits about you." I lifted myself from the boy. Taylor crawled to Pope's litter. He pulled his knees to his chest, reached out and placed his hand on his sergeant's side. The trooper, not the boy, looked at me and nodded.

June's face rested on my shoulder. The sun had fried the splash of freckles on her nose until I feared the slightest breeze could blow them away like ashes. Even her corn-silk-colored hair, always so soft in my fingers, seemed as brittle as the dried sprigs of grass around us.

I lifted the canteen to my cracked lips and pretended to take my sip of the bitter seepage we had coaxed from the cactus. Then I passed the water jug to June.

She twisted the stopper closed. "Best save this for Sergeant Pope." She was stronger than me.

Grit as fine as sugar followed the breath of wind into

the shade of the greasewood where we rested. Taylor hadn't left his sergeant's side. The other troopers hid from the noonday sun in a clump of paloverdes. Windswept particles of dirt, as if falling from a gravedigger's shovel, turned their blue uniforms gray.

"Kep, I see somethin'." June sat up and clutched the canteen to her chest. "There. Where the road crosses the ridge yonder. See the dirt in the air?"

"Just a dust devil." I wanted it to be more.

"Kep, I see a man on a horse. No, two men."

Grit scraped my eyes as I squinted to see more. June pointed to the cloud of dust on the hill. I picked out two horses and riders.

"They Apaches?" Her fingers clawed my shirtsleeve.

"No. No." I pulled myself to my feet. "Not Apaches. White men." I stepped out of the brush and waved both arms over my head. "Taylor. Look. Riders from Vengeance." I jerked the Colt from my belt and fired a shot into the air. The blast shattered the still over the desert. Taylor jumped to his feet. I fired again.

The troopers climbed from where they had rested in the brush. They waved their hats in the air. A carbine barked.

I could see clearly now. Not two riders. I counted four. And they rode toward us.

I lifted June to her feet. "Help's coming." Maybe Taylor's prayers had been answered.

"Murder raid." The leader tugged at the ends of his drooping mustache. "Victorio and more'n thirty warriors crossed up from Mexico." He took a canteen from his saddle and handed it to Taylor. "We know of two ranches they burned out south of Vengeance. Could be more we don't know about. Where'd you say they hit you?"

Taylor explained where we had been attacked.

The leader raised his hand to signal Taylor to keep his canteen. "Don't make no sense. That's farther north than we figured they'd be by now."

"Couldn't been no more than six or eight bucks in the bunch that jumped us." I took the canteen from Taylor. His eyes told me he wanted me to say more. To warn them about the wolves. I shook my head and told the cowboy, "The stage driver tried to outrun 'em but laid the coach over. They opened up on us with rifles, and while we were pinned down, they ran off the stage's team. I had a saddle horse tied to the back. They stole him. Got the troopers' horses, too."

"You only saw six or eight. Could be twice that many you didn't see." He tugged at his mustache again and rocked from foot to foot.

"Didn't actually see any. They shot at us from cover and seemed ready for any move we made." Inside I wondered if my fears and the desert heat conjured up a she-wolf with purple eyes. "Think they split off from the big bunch?"

The cowboy shook his head. "No one knows what Apaches do. Those devils attacked a stage and six cavalry carbines? Hell, that don't add up." He stared away from us and studied the desert. "I'll send one man back to Vengeance for a wagon to get y'all. We'll leave what water and food we can spare. There's three more ranches we got to get word to." The cowboy spit between his boots. "And one of 'em is mine. Got a wife and two daughters and everything I own, not three miles from where you was attacked."

"What's your name, suh?" Taylor asked.

"Joe Dupree."

"We'll pray for you, Mister Dupree."

I turned to look at June. My fingers trailed over the Colt in my belt and I remembered what Taylor had said about Apaches and white women.

"Pray these horses don't play out." Dupree swung up onto his saddle. "Most of all, you pray—" His voice cracked.

"You pray I ain't too late."

Chapter Five

Doctor Jenkins wiped his hands on a clean white rag. "Your woman told me it was you that amputated his leg. Just a jackknife, she said." He folded the rag and rubbed his fingers over a chin that looked too young to grow whiskers.

I shifted on the ladder-back chair in the office. "It was all I had. We lost everything when the Apaches burned the stagecoach."

He pulled off his spectacles and rubbed each lens in turn with the cloth. "I'm here to tell you, given what you had to work with, my instructors in medical school couldn't have done any better."

Taylor took in a deep breath. "Sergeant gonna live?"

"Now I didn't say that. No, sir. Too early to tell. He's lost a lot of blood. He's very weak." Jenkins hung his glasses back on his nose. "I tell you one thing. If you wouldn't have got his leg off, he'd be dead right now. I'm sure of that."

"Suh?"

"Don't you worry, boy. I think your sergeant is as tough as any man I've seen come through here. If anybody can make it, he will. He needs rest. I gave him some sulfa powder and whiskey. We'll just let nature take its course."

The doctor rolled his sleeves down and fastened his cuffs. "And Kepler, June, that's her name, isn't it? She fell asleep on one of the beds. You go about your business and let her sleep. My wife will look after her. We'll send word when she wakes." The young doctor scribbled a few notes on a piece of paper. "She's quite a woman. Wouldn't leave the sergeant until she was sure he was taken care of. Go on, now, get some rest for yourselves. If these Apaches have their way, none of us will rest for a long time."

And if wolves run with the Apaches—I kept the words in my brain—*none of us will ever rest again.*

———————

The troopers had found the shady side of a building on Main Street. Three empty peach cans were stacked next to the building, and the soldiers passed a full canteen among themselves. Two scraps of bread and two more cans of peaches had been set aside.

"Those for us?" Taylor nodded.

"Yes 'um," one trooper answered. "Top Sergeant?"

"Doctor's got him restin'. We just need to wait and pray."

"What we do now? We got no horses. No sergeant to tell us what."

"All I know to do is get word to the fort and see what they tell." Taylor looked at me. "Reckon?"

"I'll help you. We need to find the telegraph office." I stuffed the crust of bread in my mouth. My stomach churned with its first food. On the shaded side of Main Street, a sign marked the offices of *The Vengeance Dispatch*. A man named Thomas owned the newspaper. His letter was the reason I'd come to this town. The telegraph office sat three buildings down, and next to it, red letters on whitewash said "Cold Beer."

"C'mon, I'm buyin' you men a drink."

"Suh?"

"The saloon says it has cold beer. That sound good?"

"It does, but . . ."

"But what, Taylor? Your men earned a beer. I'll buy you all you can drink."

"Suh, some places won't let us." Taylor looked at the ground. "We be nigras."

There was only one customer in the barroom. He slumped on one table, too drunk or too asleep to care what color the soldiers were. The barkeep only cared about the color of my money. Still, Taylor and his troopers huddled around the table closest to the front door and twisted in their seats with each sound from outside. The beer that was supposed to be cold wasn't.

The troopers had finished their second mugs when the saloon doors slammed open.

"Kepler?" A man with a clipped mustache and white shirtsleeves rolled to his elbows burst in the door. "Visitin' the saloon before you come find me?"

"Sam Thomas, that how you greet your new reporter?"

"When I hear that he was almost killed before he wrote his first word, it is."

"Sit and have a beer. Meet the soldiers that brought me to Vengeance."

"Beer, hell. Bring me a whiskey and leave the bottle."

Thomas straddled a chair at the table. He pushed back his hair and left a smear of newspaper ink in the sweat on his forehead.

"Don't waste your breath tellin' me all that happened. You write me a story I can put in my paper. Told the pressman to be ready to print extra copies for tomorrow's edition. I know the way you can make words sing." The bartender set the whiskey on the table and Thomas downed it in a single gulp. He sloshed his glass full from the bottle and looked at me. "You look like somethin' that fell off a gut-wagon. Lucky to be alive, aren't you?"

I reached for his bottle and poured two fingers into my beer mug. All that had happened these past few days rushed into the barroom and perched on my shoulders. I tossed down the whiskey. Its fire did nothing to chase away the wolves that stalked somewhere behind me.

Thomas twirled his glass on the tabletop. "Heard you took up with a girl from May's place in Brokeheart. She make it?"

"She's at the doctor's. Resting."

Thomas poured his third glass of whiskey. "This country is hard on women." He poured his glass full. "My wife took my boy and caught a stage out of this God-awful town. All I can do is hang on 'til I can sell out to some poor bastard that wants to run his own newspaper as much as I did." He lifted the glass. "Take June to my house. I'm sleepin' at the office these days. Empty house is too lonesome."

"Thanks." I pointed my chin at where Taylor and his troopers waited. "Soldiers need to get a telegram off to the fort."

"I'll see to it. There's room at the paper for the four of them to sleep tonight." He drained his glass. "Somethin' tells me . . ." He didn't finish, but only stared into his empty glass.

———————————

June and I found Thomas's home in a row of white houses six blocks from Main Street. Behind the dark house sat an empty corral and a small barn. Beyond the corral there was only desert. The tips of the ragged weeds touched the fence's bottom rails.

A box of matches was on a table just inside the door where Thomas had told me it would be. I lit an oil lamp. Soft yellow took away the shadows, and June pulled close to my side.

"Back in Brokeheart," she whispered, "word got out that Miss May was good at sewin' and mendin'. Proper ladies wouldn't come to her place." Her hair brushed my arm. "They'd send word and Miss May would have me go get their things. They'd never let me come inside, but I could look through the door and see all what they had." She stepped away and touched a painting on the wall. "I told myself someday I'd live in a house like one of theirs. A house with glass windows and a parlor. Beds with enough blankets to keep you warm no matter how cold winter nights got."

June took my hand and led me into the parlor. "I'll set in a room like this one every night"—she pointed to a divan—"and read books. The books you're gonna write, Kep." She pulled my face down to hers. "Even if it ain't so, I'm gonna tell my head to believe this house is my own. Just for tonight, I will." She moved in close, and her lips grazed mine.

I let the warmth from her body melt away all my doubts about this town called Vengeance. For those seconds, Apaches stayed far away and the wolves padded off into the desert. I told my head to believe that everything would be all right.

I wanted more seconds to hold on to her, but she pulled away. "I'll find some water so you can wash yourself,

Kepler." June lifted my hands and ran the pad of her finger across my thumbnail. "You still have blood from the sergeant's leg on you."

A "tsk" sound floated up when her tongue touched her teeth.

June coaxed a fire to life in the kitchen's stove and filled a pot from the rain barrel.

Hotel rooms and boardinghouses were where I had spent my nights. I had never even thought of the comfort my own home might bring. Watching June at the stove, brewing coffee and warming wash water, doubts swirled again in my mind about bringing her here. I pushed them away.

She brought a straight razor, brush, and soap and then left me to wash up. As I scraped the desert dirt and beard from my face, I heard the rustle of a book's pages from the parlor and June's voice humming.

Chapter Six

As my pen touched the tablet the next morning at the newspaper office, I conquered my doubts and found my courage again.

I spent my energy on the heroics of Taylor and the other soldiers fending off the Apaches and guiding us through the desert to Vengeance. I introduced the readers to Sergeant Pope and his sacrifice. Any thought of wolves stayed deep inside.

Thomas put his typesetter to work and told his pressman to print an additional five hundred copies. "I want these papers on the street as soon as the ink dries." He hung a cigar in the corner of his mouth and scanned the story on the soldiers again.

"Good work, Kepler. People will pay to read this, and I just might make a few cents today. But tell me something. Why no mention that they're Buffalo Soldiers? You know— nigras."

"I didn't think it mattered."

The editor nodded. "If what we fear comes . . . the color of those trooper's skin won't matter at all."

———

That morning I bought June a new dress. She spent the afternoon at Sergeant Pope's side. I had promised to meet her at the doctor's when I had finished at the paper. As was my custom in a new town, I wandered down Main Street to get a feel for the town as a rider might do with a new horse.

Taylor and the troopers stood at the open doors of the saloon. The sounds of men's voices funneled out of the barroom.

"What's going on?" I jostled past a pair of miners on the boardwalk and grabbed the doorframe next to Taylor.

"'Member those men that found us out in the desert? Two of 'em just rode into town. They're in there now."

A crowd gathered around the two dust-covered cowboys at the bar.

"Joe Dupree, that was his name, wasn't it? Said his family was near where we'd been attacked?" I looked into the saloon.

"Yes, suh." Taylor stood aside as more men from the street rushed into the barroom. "But he ain't with 'em."

"C'mom. Let's see what this is about."

The barkeep slung two mugs of beer down the bar to the cowhands.

Both men chugged at the beer. Then the one with red hair and redder whiskers, thick with dirt, spoke. "We never saw a single Apache. Judgin' from the tracks we crossed, there was no more than five or six of 'em."

I pushed my way up to the bar and elbowed my way next to the red-haired man. "Where's Dupree and his family?" The murmur of the crowd went quiet.

The cowhand the others called Sweetwater hung his head and peered up at me with wind-dried eyes. He shook his head and looked away. "Joe split off and hightailed it for home. Billy and me were gonna make a swing and warn the other ranches. We told him we'd ride hard for his place as soon as we could."

The cowhand tapped his beer mug on the bar top. The barkeep slid another his way. "Just 'fore dark we saw the smoke. Knew right then we was too late. Billy wanted to hurry on in. I knew it was best to wait." He pinched the skin between his eyes like he was trying to trap what strength he had left inside him. "We slipped on in 'til we was maybe a mile from the house. Hid the horses and set up on a butte and watched. After sunset we could see the flames. I set up all night listenin' to wolves yowlin' and watched the fire burn itself out." He looked at the fresh beer but didn't pick it up.

The other cowboy pushed off the bar. The crowd parted, and he walked to a table and dropped heavily into a chair. "Finish the story." His hoarse whisper hung over the room.

Sweetwater pushed the mug away and rested both elbows on the bar. He studied his face in the mirror behind the bartender. As if he was talking only to himself, he whispered the rest of the story. "We waited 'til sunup. The desert was quiet as I'd ever heard. Not one bird made a noise. The house and outbuildin's was just ashes. What horses and cattle they didn't run off, they killed. Even the yard chickens was dead." He wiped his mouth on his wrist. "We found Joe's wife first. They'd—" He drained the mug and fought for the next words. "Both his girls was still in pigtails." His voice cracked with pain. "After the Apaches had their way with 'em, the wolves got to 'em. Wolf tracks and moccasin prints all over the yard. Like they was takin' turns."

"What about Joe?" My voice was the only sound in the room.

Sweetwater bobbed his head. "Musta got there after the killin' was done and the Apaches left. We could see his boot tracks near where we found his little girls. He sat down against a fence post and put his pistol to his head. Wolves never touched him. Just left their tracks in a big circle 'round his body like they was darin' us to come after them. We could hear 'em howlin' as we buried the dead." His arms dropped onto the bar and he laid his head between them.

I rattled a gold piece onto the bar. "This should cover what they drink. Get some food in 'em." I pushed my way through the crowded room and went to the Dispatch's office. I wanted to put Sweetwater's words on paper. I could tell the story no better.

Through the flyspecked front windows, a band of crimson burned along the horizon. The skies turned the color of fresh spilled blood. Shadows stretched into evening. The questions that had brought me here from Colorado swarmed in my head. Their clues were somewhere in the newspaper's office, if I could only find them.

———————

Clouds stacked over the mountains. The promise of rain scented the night air. A cool breeze hurried away the smoky haze the mines' smelter spread over Vengeance. Then raindrops stirred up the stench of the cattle pens four blocks away.

With the key Thomas had given me, I unlocked the Dispatch's front door as the rain turned to wind-driven sheets. A crack of lightning lit the office.

Thomas sprawled over his desktop, glass in hand and an empty bottle at his feet. He raised his head. "Who's there?"

"Me, Kepler."

"What time is it?"

"After ten."

He straightened in his chair and ran his hand through his hair. "Fell asleep at my desk. Workin'." The words slurred out. He rubbed at his eyes with the thumb and fingers of one hand.

I lit a pair of lanterns, and Thomas turned his face from the glare. I took an iron poker, jabbed the coals to life in the stove, and set a coffeepot to boil. "You do too much work with a whiskey bottle close by."

He shook his head. "Whatta you doin' here?"

"I'll tell you after you drink some coffee."

I sat down at my desk and scribbled out the story Sweetwater had told. Thomas turned in his chair and stared at the woodstove. Rain pelted the roof and sluiced from the eaves.

The coffee finished its brew as I put the last words on the paper. I blotted the ink and took what I had written to Thomas.

I filled two tin cups and set one next to the article. One lantern hissed, sputtered for fuel, and went dark. I moved the other closer to Thomas. He picked up his coffee, perched a pair of spectacles on the end of his nose, and began to read.

When he had finished he pushed my paper to the side of his desk and held out his cup for more of the brew. "Damn, Kepler, this is better than your story about those nigra soldiers."

"Don't put my name on it. I wrote it, but those aren't my words." While I told him about Sweetwater and Billy in the saloon, I poured both our cups full again. "The letter you sent asking me to come." I perched on a stool so I could look Thomas in the eye. "There were clippings about wolves getting to those the Apaches had killed. Just like

46

what happened to Dupree and his family. You save copies for yourself?"

Thomas pulled open the bottom drawer of his desk and lifted a sheaf of ragged pages. He let them drop on his desktop, took the top paper from the stack, and slid the rest to me. "What I sent you is in with the others."

"Others?"

"Last I counted there were near a dozen reports over a six-month span. Mostly here in Arizona. Some from over in New Mexico and two from papers down in Mexico. All the same. Apaches attack and kill some miners, or settlers or travelers. When the bodies are found, wolves have feasted on the remains."

"Why didn't you show this to me when I got here?"

He picked the whiskey bottle up off the floor and let the last drops fall into his coffee cup. He pushed the papers he had kept back across the desk. "Now's the time."

His name was printed under the headline. The few lines told of a cowhand reported missing from a nearby ranch. The body was found when a stagecoach returning to Vengeance happened upon a pack of wolves dragging something along the road. The driver had fired a shot at the animals and then discovered the grisly remains.

I looked up when I finished reading and opened my mouth to speak. He waved his hand.

"What it doesn't say there is that my wife and I were on that stage. My boy, too. We saw it all firsthand." Thomas tipped the cup and held it until the last liquid dribbled into his mouth. "My wife took the boy and was on the next stage out of this hellhole. Didn't bother to pack. Every cent I have is in this newspaper. I can't follow until I sell out."

"There was a tintype of a woman in what you sent me. Is it—"

"You'll find the picture and two others in there. The wolf attacks didn't start 'til she showed up in town."

"She's in Vengeance?" His words hit like a gut punch.

"Tomorrow, you go find Crawford Saunders. He owns the Vengeance House Hotel and half of Main Street. See what he has to say." Thomas stood. The next flash of lightning silhouetted him. He grabbed the edge of his desk to steady himself. "Remember, Kepler, if you're goin' to chase the devil, he might lead you to hell."

Thunder rumbled over Vengeance.

———————

I spent the next hours reading each of the clippings. Moans mixed with snores came from the back room where Thomas slept on his cot. As the last stroke of lightning ended the rainstorm, I placed the three pictures of the woman side by side on the desk and moved the lantern close. Each image was on faded newsprint. In one, a smudge of ink hid her face. The next was taken from behind showing only her back. In the third, as if she sensed the photograph was about to be taken, she'd turned her head, leaving only a blur of lines where her face should be. Still, in the slimness of her figure, I saw the woman from Colorado.

When weariness closed my eyes, the memory of the night she had first come to my hotel room filled all my senses. The moonlight on her skin, her breath on my face, and the way her fingers grazed the raw wound on my shoulder were as vivid now as that night last winter. When my eyes opened, the flames in the stove became the fire on the mountain that should have taken her from this world.

But Landry had come to Vengeance.

I ran, and with each stride, my boots slid in the mire the rain had made of the streets. Midnight had passed. I had forgotten to meet June at the end of the day. Sweetwater's story, newspaper clippings, and the shadowy images of Landry had stolen the minutes away.

Light slipped from the drawn shades at the back of Thomas's house. When I turned the doorknob, June met me.

Worry crowded her face. She shrank away when I reached out to touch her.

"I was at the paper." I looked down at my mud-splattered trousers. "There was a story I had to write. I'm sorry."

"There'll be another story tomorrow. And another the day after that, too." She moved farther from me. "You'll always be a stranger, Kepler. But you're safe now. That's what matters. I'm goin' to my bed. You best sleep out here tonight." She turned and left the room.

"When God took that rib from Adam's side to make Eve," my mother's words whispered in my ear as though she were standing next to me, "he would have done all womankind a favor, if he would have took just a speck of Adam's brain with it. Then we might have just a clue on how each other thinks. Men and women want each other. We need each other, we surely do. But we'll never truly understand one another."

I could stare at a blank sheet of paper and my mind would bring just the right words to my pen. But standing in the borrowed house and watching June walk down the hall filled me with confusion. Since the day I left my mother's home to find my way in the world, I had concerned myself with only myself. Responsibilities were avoided. Relationships used to advantage. Fortunes never shared.

Even as the news hit me of Landry here in Vengeance, it was my name on the byline that first filled my thoughts, not the evil that must be stopped.

Perhaps June and I would always be strangers.

Maybe I wanted it that way.

At first light, I went to the bedroom where June slept. I sat on the edge of the bed and bent my face toward hers. Her eyes never opened. I kissed her cheek and left to find the next sliver of truth about Landry.

Chapter Seven

The rain had cleaned the air. Puddles filled the wheel ruts in Main Street. Mud formed in the shade of the storefronts and adobe corrals, but where the desert sun baked the dirt, clouds of dust lifted around my boots. Three men sat on the boardwalk in front of the saloon where Sweetwater had told his terrible story last night. Burros loaded with picks and shovels stood tied to the rail. Their tails flicked at the swarms of flies that buzzed around them.

"Word of Apaches runnin' wild brought us in from the hills and we're thirsty," one man shouted as I passed. "When does this barroom open?"

"Bang hard on that door," I told him. "Heard the man that runs the place sleeps under the billiard table. If he's like any other barkeep west of Denver, he won't miss the chance to take your money."

A wagon driven by a bleary-eyed man slopped through the rain puddles. A more-tired woman sat next to the driver. What seemed to be everything they owned was heaped in the wagon bed. Their cart never slowed as it rumbled past.

At the end of the street, a boy tugged on a horse's lead rope, urging the animal onto Main from a cross street shaded by the steeple of a church. When the passing wagon flung muddy water their way, the horse tossed its head and tried to pull away.

I caught the rope and settled the horse. "You handle this one by yourself?"

"I can, Mister." He picked at a crusty scab on his nose.

"Where you taking him?"

"Down to the livery. My pa gave me money to pay the man to keep 'im in his corrals." He touched the pocket of his worn pants.

"Why's your pa sending you?"

"He stayed at the ranch and made ma and me come to town." He tugged on the lead rope, reached up, and stroked the white blaze on the horse's nose. "On account of the Apaches."

"Where's your ma?"

"She's stayin' with the wagon and some other folks by that big church. Preacher said we can camp there. How much you think that man'll want to watch a horse? Ain't got but a few pennies."

"What's your name, boy?"

"Fum Davis."

"Fum?"

"Yes, sir. My ma named me after an uncle back in Missouri. His name is a real long word. When I was learnin' to talk I couldn't get my tongue to say it." He whisked a fly from the horse's muzzle. "As much as I tried, it just came out Fum."

"Tell you what, Fum." I tangled my fingers in his horse's mane. "There's an empty corral behind the house where I'm staying. You put your horse there and save your pennies for you and your ma."

"You think that'd be all right?" He studied my face. "My pa trusted me with this horse."

"And he trusted you with his money, too?"

"Yes, sir." His tongue touched his lips.

"Then I think he'd want you to do what's best."

"I think Pa would want me to pay somethin'. It's only right, ain't it?"

"Then give one of your pennies to the lady at the house." I told Fum how to find Thomas's place. "The lady's name is June. Tell her Kepler sent you."

Fum's face turned stern as if he were considering the best deal he could for his family. Then he put out his hand to shake mine. "Thank you, Mister Kepler." He scooted his boot through the mud. "Lookee that." He tapped a muddy spot where the boardwalk shaded the dirt.

Pressed into the wet earth, an animal's footprint was plain.

"Seen those near our ranch"—Fum touched the toe prints with his fingers—"wolf track for sure. You suppose an old wolf walked right down the main street of this town?"

I drew a circle on the inside of my cheek with my tongue. "Fum, best get your horse to that corral."

I waited until the boy and his horse had crossed Main Street before I examined the marks in the mud. No other tracks marred the soil around it. Except for Fum's fingerprints, the track was untouched. The animal had left the print after last night's rain.

Rounded, muddy smudges mixed with the boot prints on the boardwalk's wooden slats. I imagined a gray she-wolf creeping along the storefronts last night.

In the next block sat the Vengeance House Hotel. Just the place I was headed.

"Rooms are all taken." The man behind the hotel counter never looked up from the newspaper he was reading. "Got some old mattresses I spread out in the halls. Those go for five dollar a night. If you sleep on the floor that'll cost ya three. And you'll pay up front, you will. Don't like it, get on down the street."

"I'm not looking for a room. I need to talk to Crawford Saunders."

"Then get to talkin'." He let the paper rest on the counter and looked up. His hair was almost white, and his skin seemed no thicker than a page from the Bible. Wrinkles from too many days in the desert sun lined his face. When he rubbed the corner of his mouth, blue veins corded the back of his hand. He looked me over, and a spark of interest bloomed in his eyes. "You're that new reporter fella, aren't you? Just reading somethin' you wrote. I liked it."

"Thank you."

"You gonna write about me?"

My mother had taught me that a quarter turn on the truth worked better than a flat lie. "I'm planning on it."

Saunders folded the newspaper and pushed it aside. He licked his thumb and ran it over the vein-like crack in the wooden countertop.

Mother said to praise a man at every chance if you want something. Her praises bought a laundry and a boarding-house back home.

I smiled my best smile. "Townfolks tell me that if anything happens in Vengeance, you're the first to know."

"I should. I sit on the town council, you know."

"Someone mentioned that."

He smoothed the brambles that were his eyebrows. "Been in this town near twenty-eight years, I have. Came when this was nothin'. Own this hotel, seven other buildin's on Main Street, and have a share in the bank and the smelter. A man owns that much has need to know what happens before it does."

A cloud of dust from a wagon on Main Street floated in through the open door. Saunders pointed. "See there, another wagonload of settlers comin' to town 'cause they fear the Apaches."

I took a scrap of paper and a pencil stub from my shirt pocket. I printed Saunders's name across the paper in block letters. He glanced down. I turned that paper slightly so he could see what I had written.

He nodded and began to speak. "Last count there was thirty-five hundred people in Vengeance, not counting Mexicans and tame Indians. There'll be another eight hundred here 'fore day's end. And half again as many tomorrow. Apaches got everyone spooked." Saunders tapped the paper. "You gonna write that down, aren't ya?"

I wrote the three-five-oh-oh in letters just smaller than Saunders's name. "You don't think the Apaches will attack Vengeance, do you?"

He stroked his chin to show me he was mulling over my question. "Most likely, no. They'll raid some ranches, run off as many horses and cows as they can. A few unfortunates will get their throats cut. Then the army will chase 'em back into Mexico. Next year or the year after they'll do the same thing, just like before."

"I've heard this is different than the other times."

Saunders lowered his voice. "You mean the talk about the wolves?"

"You've heard that too?"

"Yup."

"And?"

"And do I believe that Apaches turn into wolves and eat the bodies of what they kill?"

"Do you?"

"In this country you don't *not* believe anything." He dug into the crack in the wood with his thumbnail. "Kepler, that your name, isn't it?"

"It is."

"That your given name?" He examined the bit of grime that clung to his thumb.

"Folks just call me Kepler."

"Well, Kepler, you know why this town is called Vengeance?"

I shook my head.

He flicked the speck of dirt away. "Apaches tell a story—a myth, a legend, whatever you call it—about before white men ever came to this God-awful country. Seems their warriors was all away raidin' or huntin'." He touched the paper as if he wanted me to write. "Spanish conquistadors raided their village. Killed the women. Old folks. Claimed they even smashed the heads of newborn babies against rocks. Done terrible, unthinkable things." He tapped the paper again. "Get this part down, now. When the warriors come back and find the massacre, they go after the Spaniards. They track 'em day and night. For days. They lose the trail, then this here she-wolf appears—all magic-like—and leads 'em to the Spaniards."

I scribbled down a few words and looked up at Saunders.

"The legend claims them conquistadors camped right in this here valley. The she-wolf leads the Apaches down the mountainside and they take their revenge. Murder every single Spaniard. To show their thankfulness to the wolf, the Apaches feed her the hearts of all those they killed." Saunders drew in a breath and waited until I looked at his face. "Some of those hearts was still beatin', the story goes. That's why the place where this town sits got called Vengeance."

Saunders smiled as if he were proud of the way he'd told the story. "There's one more part, now. The Apaches claim that sometime in the future, it's all gonna happen again. A she-wolf is gonna lead them back here to take revenge on their enemies. But this time when they attack, *all*"—he wagged his eyebrows—"the Apaches are gonna change into wolves. And feast on their enemies' hearts."

I looked down at the cracked counter. "Do you believe any of that is true?" I thought of the wolves that circled the crippled stagecoach that night in the desert.

"I believe that the Apaches believe it's true. Get enough whiskey in 'em and they might *really* believe it."

"And?"

"Like I said, there'll be near four thousand in town in two days. More than half of those'll be men with rifles. Let 'em come. We can be right nasty." From under the counter Saunders pulled out a cut-down Winchester. The old man winked.

I nodded, more to give me time to think through what Saunders had just told me than to show approval.

"When that there gonna be in the paper, Kepler?"

"I'll discuss it with my editor. Decisions on what to print are his." I reached into my pocket, took out the pictures Thomas had given me, and laid them before Saunders. "One more thing. I'm trying to find this woman."

"I know her." Saunders barely glanced at the picture.

"She showed up in Vengeance one night maybe a year ago. Rented her a room I did. She wanted the best I had."

"Do you know where she is now?"

"That's the peculiar part." He pushed away from the counter and stood for the first time. He picked up a homemade crutch and propped it under his arm. His left leg was missing below the knee. A footless pant leg swept along the floor. "She paid me up front for six months. Paid in shiny new twenty-dollar gold pieces. Not a scratch on 'em. Six months come and she walks in here one night, just before I was gonna close things up, and pays for another six months. Just like before. Shiny new gold, never silver."

"Did you have her sign the hotel register?" I eyed the book on the counter.

Saunders covered the register with his hands. "One of her stipulations was that she didn't. I don't argue with gold."

"So she's here now?"

"Don't know. She's peculiar, that one. Pretty enough to take a man's breath away and make him start thinkin' things." He shook his head. "Somethin' sure strange about her. Comes and goes. Maid goes in to clean the room. Sometime it's never touched. Sometime it's as dusty as a stable." He let his weight slump on his crutch. "I think she's prospectin' out in the desert, I do. Though she don't look like no miner."

"When was the last time she was here?"

"Maybe a week." He squinted his eyes. "Yeah, just about a week. Just heard about you bein' here in town, and the maid told me her room had been used. Didn't see her myself, though." He scratched his head, and his eyes brightened with a thought. "Tonight I just might check that room to see if she's gonna be here. If not, I can rent it out to some sorry traveler runnin' from the Apaches. That's good business, it is."

"When will you check?"

"'Bout midnight."

"Mind if I stop by?"

"Suit yourself."

I turned to leave and Saunders added, "You're not the first one to ask about that woman."

"Oh?" I turned back and took hold of the counter with both hands.

"Little towheaded gal I seen you with came in here last night during the rainstorm. Pretty, she was. Asked if a European woman ever stayed here."

"And?"

"Told her some of what I just told you." His eyebrows arched. "Thought she would have told you about it."

Chapter Eight

Grit kicked up from wagons on Main Street caked between my fingers and left its taste on my tongue. It would be near midnight before the day's heat broke.

I found Taylor and one of his Buffalo Soldiers resting in the shade in front of the marshal's office. Their tattered uniforms had been laundered, and full cartridge belts hung from their hips.

Taylor jumped to attention. "Mister Kepler, suh."

"Your orders come from the fort?"

"Yes, suh. Telegraph say a detachment comin' in with the mine's payroll wagon. We supposed to wait for them. Meantime, we to help the marshal."

"Sergeant Pope?"

"Better, suh. Miss June sets with him most of each day. Sergeant, he still sleeps a lot, but he's eatin' hard food now."

"The doctor said if anyone could make it, it would be him."

"Our prayin' helped him, too."

Three cowhands dodged their lathered horses around the wagons on the street. They tied their mounts at the rail in front of the saloon and jostled shoulders to be the first through the door.

"Been comin' in all mornin'." Taylor whistled through his teeth. "When they ain't in the saloons, them cowboys hang out at the corrals. Settler families campin' over at the big white church. Apaches got 'em all scared. I don't know, suh."

"What's that?"

Up the street another wagon rolled into town.

"Not sure God intended people to bunch up this close together. Some of those cowboys are awful hard-lookin' men. Get too many roosters in the chicken yard"—he spit on the ground—"bound to be trouble."

I nodded at what he said. "Hear anything else?"

"They say some of the small ranchers are gatherin' what few cows they got into a big herd. Gonna bring 'em to town. Maybe by tonight."

I thought of Fum's father. "Figure they have a better chance in one big bunch than each trying on his own?"

"Reckon."

"Where you off to?"

"Marshal wants us to walk the streets so people know we around. You?"

"I think I'll head over to the church. If I ask enough people enough questions I usually find a story." And it would keep my mind away from what I might find upstairs in the hotel room tonight.

"God be with you, Kepler." Taylor picked up his carbine. He and the other soldier walked down the street.

I knew June would be at the doctor's with Pope. But it would be best to ask about Landry when we could be alone. For now there was a story to hunt.

———

"Fumberly!"

I would not have expected such a big voice could come

from such a small woman. Her head barely reached the top of the wagon's wheel. She wiped her hands on a stained apron, gathered her skirts, and strode across the churchyard. Desert sun and countless washings had faded any color from her dress.

"Fumberly," she hollered out again and the camp went quiet. The woman lifted her hair so the breeze could cool the back of her neck. "Boy, I told you no playin' 'til your chores was done."

In three running steps, Fum caught up to a rolling iron wheel rim. He stabbed at the hoop with a stick, and the circle of rusty metal toppled to the ground.

"Hello, Fum," I said and tipped my hat to his mother.

The boy smiled. "Ma, this is Mister Kepler. He's the one I told you about. Made that deal with him to keep the horse in his corral."

His mother gathered the sides of her skirt in her hands and tilted her head forward in a half curtsy. "Pleased to meet you." In one motion, she caught her son by the shirt collar before he could move away. "Fum, you catch that nanny goat and milk it, like I told you. Poor woman in that wagon's got a newborn and needs our help. Be quick about it." She pushed him away.

Fum stuffed his hands in his pockets. He scuffed his feet through the dirt, took a tin pail from their wagon, and stomped out to a patch of grass where the goat was tied.

His mother watched him for a moment, one hand touching her eyes, and even in the heat of day, a shiver coursed through her body. "I surely love that boy," she said more to herself than to me. She turned. "I do want to thank you for letting us keep our horse at your place. When my husband gets to town he'll thank you too." Dampness filled her red-rimmed eyes.

"It was the right thing to do."

"Your woman, June, walked back with Fum. She tried to give me the penny back. I wouldn't take it. I told her that was between you and Fumberly." She smiled when she said her son's name.

"You can do me a favor, Missus Davis."

"What's that?"

"Introduce me to some of the other folks 'round here. I might find a story for the paper."

"I'd be happy to. Already made new friends with these folks. And you'll want to talk to my husband. He'll be in with the other men and the cattle. Tonight." She looked out into the desert and supped up a breath. "Can't think no other way."

———————

Sun blazed down and glared from the upstairs windows of The Vengeance House. Fum's mother watched the skyline for any sign of her husband, the herd of cattle, and the other men. For both of us, the sun moved too slowly.

I learned what I could from the little band of women, old men, and children camped in the churchyard. All watched the desert for their men to come in with the cattle. When I walked back to the newspaper office, I watched for wolf tracks in the dust along Main Street. I found none.

June fixed a supper of greens and venison. In the burnished light of dusk, we ate on the porch of Thomas's home. Silence sat there with us. When the minutes stretched, I started to apologize for the previous night. June cut me short. She gave me a long account of her day with Sergeant Pope. Her hand rested where the fabric of her new dress gathered across her stomach. I watched it rise and fall with each breath she took.

"June, I heard you stopped at the hotel last night."

She nodded. "Doctor's wife told me she saw this fancy lady sneaking up the back stairs late one night. All I could think of was the lady what killed my cat in Brokeheart. It's her, isn't it?" Her eyes begged me not to lie.

"I'm going to try to find out for sure tonight, but I think it's her."

"Then what you do? Write a big story? Or stop her?"

"Couldn't it be both?"

"Just stop her, Kep." June shifted from where she sat on the porch steps. "Kepler, hear that?"

The sound of faraway hoofbeats drifted in on the wind. "It's the cattle. Those settlers must be bringin' their herd in." I took her hand, and my fears of Landry fled. We hurried to the hope of Main Street.

A speckled heifer with a broken horn led the parade. People lined the boardwalks. The fears that hung over Vengeance lifted for the first time in days as confused cattle milled about in the street. Dusty riders popped rope ends in the air and hurried the cows to the corrals at the end of the street. In spite of the wet marks that traced Fum's mother's face, a smile beamed when she saw her husband.

Fum dashed from the crowded boardwalk. His father caught his arm and swung the boy onto the back of his saddle. Fum pressed his face onto his father's back and his arms squeezed the man's waist.

"Them cows ain't much to look at." June pointed at the herd and leaned her back against my chest. "All spindly-legged and skinny. Ain't like there's one good beefsteak on the whole lot of 'em."

"They're all those people have."

I took an inventory of my possessions. My mother's pistol, two changes of clothes, money in a Denver bank. A borrowed house, no horse, and a silver bullet. "When you have little, you take care of it." I turned June's face to mine. "About Landry—"

She faced me, reached up, and placed two fingers across my lips. My hands found her hips. Once again, mother whispered in my thoughts. "Never look for the simple way. Dig deep when other men scrape the top. Find the right." June's eyes spoke the same lesson.

We stood with the crowd of wives and children and watched the cattle move by. Cowhands drifted out of the saloons. Some found their horses and joined the settlers with their herd.

Bonfires were set in the churchyard. From the edge of the firelight, we watched until the night wrapped all around us. Hoarded food began to cook. One by one, riders returned from the corrals and found their families in the camp. Family groups blended together. Steaming bowls of stew were shared with the cowhands who'd helped. Music from a mouth harp joined a fiddle. With other couples, Fum's mother danced with his father.

Taylor wandered up to where we sat. "God been good to these people today." He sat on his heels and watched the settlers' party with us.

I wrapped an arm around June's waist. "Nobody would say it out loud, but we all wondered if they'd make it in before the Apaches or something else . . ."

Taylor shifted his rifle in his hands. "Kepler, somethin'

you should know. Heard 'em talkin' down by the corrals. One of them ranchers say that last night when they had all the cattle gathered together, a pack of wolves moved in real close. Didn't threaten nobody. Just sat and watched. And this mornin' those wolves trailed 'em most of the way on into Vengeance." The boy rubbed the soft stubble on his chin. "Like the ones we saw out at the stagecoach."

Chapter Nine

The bonfire in the settlers' camp burned to red embers. Fum fell asleep against a wagon wheel with a half eaten bowl of stew spilled over his pants. His mother and father sat a few steps from him, staring into the glowing ashes. His mother's head rested on her husband's shoulder.

"We should go now." June stood from where we had watched the settlers celebrate. She took my hand and urged me to my feet. "This is their time, now. We shouldn't be awatchin'." She didn't say a word about the Apaches and wolves that I knew might come with the new day.

Taylor rested his carbine over his shoulder and walked with us. We slipped from the churchyard to Main Street as quietly as the smoke wisped away from the dying campfire.

Propped by his crutch, one-legged Crawford Saunders waited at the door of his hotel. In a voice just loud enough to hear, he called to me: "Got a man what wants that room if she ain't in it. If you're still wantin' to see her room, I'm fixin' on goin' up there." He scooted the crutch across the rough boards. "Comin'?"

I let loose June's hand. "I need to go now." I wanted to tell her not to worry. That I'd be home soon. Instead I told her, "Taylor will walk you home."

"When you be home?"

"I can't be sure." I hated having to say that.

"Then find your story, Kep." Her fingers found the corner of her eyes and she walked away.

Oil lamps sputtered and popped in the hotel lobby. In the garish haze, two cowhands stretched out on the floor. Their heads rested on their saddles. A ragged snore vibrated from one man. His friend jabbed the sleeping man's ribs, but the noise only rattled louder.

"Got another place I can sleep, Saunders?" The cowboy took another poke at his friend.

"Every room's taken, and people sleepin' in the halls upstairs." Saunders hobbled to the snorer and poked at the man's stomach with his crutch. The man rolled onto his side. A tremor rumbled up from deep in his throat. Saunders jabbed again. "How much whiskey this one drink?"

The cowhand rubbed his head. "No way of tellin'. Got to celebratin' about the settlers comin' in with their cattle." He glared down at his snoring friend. "Give me my two dollars and I'll go sleep in the street."

"No refunds," Saunders spit out.

The cowhand clamped his hands over his ears and settled back onto the pillow of his saddle's seat.

A voice came from a dark corner of the lobby. "When are you going to know if you have a room for me?" A barrel-chested man in a bowler hat and white shirt shifted on an upholstered chair.

"Fixin' on findin' that right now." Saunders turned to me. "Watch where you're steppin'"—he winked at me—"don't want to hurt no payin' customers."

Saunders grabbed the railing with one hand,

balanced his crutch in the other, and hopped up the stair-case. I followed.

A man curled in a ball slept on the first landing. Muted coughs and the sounds of clearing throats punched through the stale odors that filled the hallway.

Saunders whispered, "I told that drummer man in the lobby he could have the room if she ain't there." Even in the dark I saw his eyes flash. "Gonna charge him twenty-five dollars, I will."

At the room closest to the top of the stairway, Saunders pressed his ear to the door. "Don't hear nothin'; she must not be in there."

He fumbled in his coat pocket for the key.

"Knock," I whispered.

"What's that?" he hissed back.

"Knock before you open it. She could be asleep." If monsters ever slept. My fingers found the pistol on my hip. I slipped it from my belt. Letting it hang in my hand beside my leg, I pulled the hammer back.

"Landry?" I pushed by Saunders and rapped my knuckles on the painted wood. I wanted the creature to rise up as the door opened. I wanted the silver bullet under the hammer of my cocked pistol to tear into her. To end it all now. I tapped again. "Landry?"

Saunders put the key into the lock and turned it. The door swung inward. Cool air washed over my face.

"Hot damn, she ain't here." Saunders shuffled away from the door toward the stairs.

"Wait. I'll pay the twenty-five dollars."

"Huh?" Saunders stopped.

"You heard me. I'll pay what you're asking for the room. Send the drummer somewhere else."

Saunders rubbed his chin. "He said he'd take it tomorrow night, too. You pay for that?"

"I said I'll give you twenty-five. Light the lantern."

"Gimme the money first."

I dug into my vest pocket for the coins. "The light."

Saunders scooped the money from my palm. He hitched the crutch under his arm and hobbled to a chest of drawers against the wall.

Like a ghost come stirring to life, the window curtain waved in the darkness. Saunders's match scraped over the bureau's top. A spark snapped. In the ring of light from the match, I saw the bed in the shadowy dark. In another second the oil wick caught and light bathed the room.

Saunders turned from the oil lamp and leaned on his crutch. "Bed ain't been slept in." He hobbled to the center of the room. "Don't know why that window's open. I told the woman that makes up the rooms to be sure it was shut, on account of all this dust from the wagons."

I lowered the hammer on my pistol and slipped it back into my belt. Relief should have rushed in, but my stomach knotted.

Saunders pulled open a dresser drawer. "Her things are here." His gnarled fingers trailed across the garments. "All frilly and nice. High dollar, I'm guessin'."

I searched for something to prove that more than a woman used the room. I wanted to see scraps of animal hide and bits of bones, but the hairbrush on the dresser, the clothes, the unused bed seemed to shout that the demon I feared had never set foot here.

"Look at this dress." The old man clucked his tongue. On the back of the door hung a long, pale gray gown. It shimmered like a dove's breast in the flame's light.

"I'm guessin' it's made of silk. Ain't much to it. It'd hang fine on a woman like that one, it would." He caught the bedpost and tottered to the open window. "Judas priest, look here. The window must been open all last night. Rained in, it did. Mud all over my floor." He took hold of the window sash.

I grabbed his wrist before he could close the window. The breeze tangled the curtain around my arm. A wolf track, like the one Fum had found on the street, marked the dust spots on the window sill. The toes pointed in.

"Stand back." I pushed Saunders.

He fell onto the bed. "What the hell, Kepler?"

I grabbed the oil lamp from the bureau and brought it to the window. As the yellow light touched the floor, it was plain that our boot prints smudged over other tracks in the damp dirt. But at the edge of the smear, a woman's bare footprint was clear. The knots in my stomach pulled tighter.

From outside, pistol shots snapped near the churchyard. Voices shouted. Above the commotion, an animal screamed in pain. I pushed back the curtains. A spray of orange sparks rose from the fire pit in the settler's camp. New wood caught fire and flames blazed.

"What is it?" Saunders pulled himself to the window.

"I'm not sure." I leaned out. My hand touched the wolf's track on the sill.

Women and children huddled close to the fire. Men grabbed rifles. One pointed into the dark.

"Fumberly!" his mother screamed from far away.

I dove out the window, rolled across the roof, caught the edge with my hands, and hit the ground running.

———————

The boy was in his mother's arms when I reached the camp.

He trembled no matter how tightly she held him.

"What happened?" I bent over, grabbed my knees, and drew in as much air as I could.

"Wolf," his mother whispered.

My lungs stopped. Like the wheezing sound from a torn hole in a blacksmith's bellows I hissed, "Tell me what happened."

Fum's father, with a Winchester still in his hands, stepped into the circle of firelight. "I sent Fum to bring his nanny goat in for the night. As soon as he left, a gray wolf dashed through here, close enough to reach out and touch. Not a bit scared of the fire or the people. I thought it was after Fum. At the last second it leaped over him and caught the goat by the throat. Some cowboy got off a couple shots but it was gone." The voice of the man who braved the Apaches to bring in the few cows he owned broke. "I thought I'd lost my boy." He wrapped his arms around his wife and son.

Other settlers gathered around the family.

"Did anyone see where the wolf came from?" I asked the group.

Fum's mother raised her hand and pointed toward Main Street. "I swear it came from the roof of that hotel."

———————

"I ordered that bunch of Buffalo Soldiers to watch the corrals." The marshal paced his office floor for the third time. "If there's a wolf hunting in town, I thought we should keep watch over the livestock. I don't want a bunch of drunk cowboys down there with guns.

Saunders reached out and blocked the man's path with his crutch. "Stand still, will ya? We need to decide what to do and we need to do it quick." He looked around the lawman's office at the other members of the town council.

"That wolf must have hydraphobie." A red-faced man in a rumpled shirt started to stand. He looked at Saunders and sat back in his chair. "That's be the only reason why it ain't scared of people. Only reason."

"I heard one of those settlers say a pack of wolves followed the herd into town," the man who owned the saloon said. "Stayed just a rifle shot away. Maybe there's more of 'em."

Saunders pointed the end of his crutch at me. "Kepler, what do you know?"

If I told what I suspected, they'd call me a fool. If I didn't, more than a goat would be dead. I sucked in a breath.

Thomas spoke before I could say anything. "The goat was killed by a wolf, I'm sure of it. Tore open its windpipe and snapped its neck. That wolf, or whatever it was, coulda killed a boy instead of a goat, from the way the settlers tell it. Kepler and I took a torch and looked for tracks in every alley and street between there and the edge of town. Nothing. If it was a wolf we can't prove it. I won't publish a story in my newspaper with nothing more than that."

"I want to hear Kepler." Saunders pounded his crutch on the floor like a gavel.

I looked at the men in the room and measured my words. I could have told them about the wolf track in the hotel room, the track Fum had showed me in the street, the pack that surrounded the stage, and things I knew from

Colorado. Instead, I said, "Like Thomas said, we didn't find any tracks."

Saunders looked hard at me. "That all?"

"That's all."

He shook his head. "As head of the town council, I move that we put a two-dollar bounty on every wolf pelt brought in. If there's a rabid wolf around, somebody's bound to kill it." The men nodded. "And that we encourage Thomas and Kepler not to put anything in the paper that will rile things up. People got enough to worry about with the Apaches. All agreed?"

The men in the room murmured their approval.

"One more thing, Kepler." Saunders stared at me. "I'm gonna say this in front of everyone here. I'm an old man, but I know how to read people. I'd wager there's somethin' you ain't sayin'."

Every man in the room looked at me.

Saunders went on. "When things get tight and lives are on the line, some men wonder what they're gonna do." He licked his lips. "And some wonder what they've done." He struggled up from his chair and balanced on his one leg. "I can't figure what kind you are."

Chapter Ten

Thomas put me to work writing an article for a single page he intended to have on the street at first light. The town council had warned us not to print anything about the wolf attack that might alarm the swelling town. I chose to tell of the ranchers who brought the herd to town to save their precious animals from the Apaches, the celebration that followed as families united, and the courage those men displayed.

In the pressroom, Thomas laid out the poster that would be on the back of my story, announcing the two-dollar bounty to be paid on wolves.

When I finished, I set the type and we both slung ink and paper until the sun rose. All the while, the image of the muddy footprint on the floor of Landry's empty room was as close to me as my next breath. Each time I bent to gather the next sheaf of paper, I checked the windows.

Thomas gave the papers to Taylor and the other Buffalo Soldiers to distribute around Vengeance. I drifted off to sleep at my desk.

June woke me. She brought fresh biscuits on her way to sit with Sergeant Pope. When she looked in my eyes, I turned away. I'd left her alone for another night.

"Somethin' down at the corrals you should see, Kepler." Thomas rolled down the sleeves of his shirt. "One of

Taylor's troopers told me about it while I was handing out papers."

"What is it?"

"Just come. They're waitin' for us."

Thomas led me down Main Street, past a dozen store-fronts and as many saloons. We stopped at the corrals and stables near the outskirts of town. The settlers' cattle milled in a trampled pasture. Flies hung as thick in the hot air as the smell of fresh manure. The air seemed alive with the buzz of their wings.

Thomas pointed at a far corral. "Some drifter brought that string of horses in late yesterday. He sold them for drinkin' money. Look close, now. I'd swear one of them is the horse that was saved from the stable fire in Leadville a year ago. Your horse, Kepler."

I pulled away from Thomas and raced around the corrals.

The white-faced roan's ears perked. He pushed his way through the other horses in the enclosure and met me at the fence. The Indian that helped me name Seer had told me that horses with two different colored eyes could see the spirits that walk the earth. Many times Seer had proved that.

I tangled my fingers in his mane. "June will be glad I've found you, boy," I whispered just loud enough for the horse to hear.

Thomas climbed up the rail fence and reached out to touch the horse. "You lose him when the Apaches attacked?"

"Yeah, they got him when they ran off the stage's team." I touched my forehead to the horse's face. "Thought I'd never see him again."

"Look there"—he pointed—"the others that fella

brought in have the stage line's brand. And that black gelding has a US mark on its flank."

Taylor swung up onto the top rail. "That be Sergeant Pope's horse."

My fingers found Seer's soft muzzle, and I bit down on my lip. "Let's see if we can find the man who sold these horses."

"Where are you goin' to look?"

"You said he was needin' drinkin' money."

Thomas smiled for the first time that morning. "I could use a drink myself."

———

I made a deal with the stable owner for Seer and Pope's black gelding and had the horses moved to stalls in the barn. He told us the man he'd bought the horses from was slight, had a pockmarked, hatchet face, and wore his hair in braids.

"You get a name?" I asked him.

"Didn't have to." The stableman shook his head. "Seen his face on a Mexican wanted poster a while back. He's called Little Jed."

Thomas grabbed my arm. "Kepler, if it's the man I'm thinkin' about, Little Jed stood eyeball to eyeball with Doc Holliday on this town's Main Street two months ago and Holliday backed down."

My next breath caught in my throat. I turned back to Seer so Thomas wouldn't see my doubt. "What was John Henry Holliday doin' in Vengeance?" I bluffed.

"Passin' through on his way to meet up with the Earp brothers in Tombstone. But that has nothin' to do with this. Little Jed is trouble."

I touched the pistol hidden on my hip. "You still want a drink, don't you?"

The musk from a fresh-killed animal tinged the air. We stepped from the sunshine of the street into the shadows of the saloon. Bits of hair and smears of blood trailed across the rough wooden floorboards. A dozen men gathered at one end of the rough-hewn bar. Bottles and glasses sat on empty tables, as if everyone in the saloon had rushed to see the display on the bar top.

The skin of a charcoal-colored wolf stretched out over the wooden planks. I pushed my way into the crowd. "Where'd you kill it?" I wanted to reach out and run my fingers through the thick fur, but my hand refused to touch it.

A bearded man from the middle of the group shouted, "On the road between here and the minds. Heard about the bounty and went out mid-mornin'. Didn't think we'd see anything 'til nightfall. This here one came to us."

"What do you mean by that?"

"It came lopin' along the creek bottom right at us. Somethin' had 'im spooked. Never seen a wolf more worried on what was behind it than what was in front. And look here." He lifted the hide from the bar. Dark drops of blood dripped from the pelt, and the tip of the beast's tail coiled around a spittoon on the floor. "Got fresh teeth on its butt-end like it got into a fight with somethin' and had to get away quick." He dropped the skin, upended a whiskey glass, and then smacked the empty on the bar. "What you suppose could run off a devil the size of this 'un?"

I thought of the wolf that leaped from the hotel roof,

killed a boy's goat, and disappeared. And wolf tracks that changed to a woman's footprint. In the crowded hot saloon, an icy fingertip of doubt grazed my spine. A hunter's bullet could not kill what I feared. It would take the silver one loaded in my revolver. The town's bounty would do little good.

A big man I recognized from the town council meeting filled the talker's glass. Taylor elbowed his way to the bar so he could see the wolf's skin. The bartender eyed both of us. "Whacha needin'?"

"Cold beer for the soldiers." I dropped folded bills on the bar and jerked a thumb at the table where the other troopers sat.

The barkeep looked over my shoulder at the men at the bar. "I'll get you a beer, but . . ."

A sharp-faced man stepped out of the group at the bar. He hooked his thumbs in his gun belt. "But, he don't serve their *kind* in here." Greasy strands of braided hair hung to his shoulders. Blood pulsed behind an old scar that puckered the skin over his right eye.

"Now, Little Jed"—the man behind the bar eased back until his hips touched the sideboard—"let me give 'em a beer and they can be on their way. They just came in to see the wolf. That's all."

Little Jed's tongue traced the corners of his mouth. "I intend on settin' at one of your tables until I ride out of here in the mornin', and I don't want to chance touchin' my lips to a glass one of *them* drank out of."

I let my left arm hang at my side but lifted my right hand to rub the stubble on my chin. All the other men at the bar stared at their glasses. If anything would happen, it would be between Little Jed and me. "Now, friend"—I dropped my hand from my chin to my chest and strummed my fingers on my shirt—"these soldiers saved my life. Two just like them were killed by Apache bullets, and their sergeant, right this minute, is lyin' in the doctor's bed." My hand edged down my shirt, closer to the revolver tucked behind my hip.

Little Jed moved within an arm's length of me. Strings of spittle hung from his broken teeth. "Then I need to talk to the doctor 'bout boilin' them sheets. Nigra should be in the stable with the other animals."

The spittoon rattled across the floor. The line of men moved away from the bar. Behind me, chairs squeaked.

"Get their kind out of here now." Jed slid his hand along the top of his belt toward his holster.

My muscles coiled rattlesnake tight. Jed's fingers touched his Colt. With no time to grab my gun, I struck out, snatched a whiskey bottle from the bar, and smashed it into the side of the bigot's face.

My left hand caught his wrist as he clawed for his pistol. Strength met strength. I caught his knee on the front of my thigh as it jabbed for my groin. Tossing my weight forward, we wrestled against the bar and onto the wolf's pelt. His feet slid out from under him on the bloody floor. The heavy fur slipped from the bar, and Jed fell with it into the puddle of blood, beer, and slime from the overturned spittoon. My fingers clamped tighter on his gun hand, twisting his wrist until his gun dropped away.

I pressed the jagged neck of the whiskey bottle to Little Jed's throat. "Barkeep"—I let it cut until a trickle of blood dripped from Jed's neck to the floor—"beer for the soldiers."

The beat of Jed's heart raced behind the scar over his eye. "Kill me now or this'll never be over."

I twisted the shard of glass until the top layer of Jed's flesh tore. "You're not worth it." Pressing my knee into his chest, I stood up and kicked his pistol across the floor toward Taylor.

Taylor grabbed it up and pointed the gun at the line of men. "We waitin' for our beer, suh."

Dragging his back along the floor, Little Jed scrambled away from me. He pulled his feet under him and wiped his hand along his throat. "You'll pay for this." A crooked smile twisted his mouth, and he licked his own blood from his fingers. "You'll pay." Jed tapped his empty holster, pointed his finger at me, and snapped his thumb down. He backed out of the doors and onto the street.

Every grain of sand that coated my dirty skin stood on end. My mother's words echoed in the back of my brain: "Beat a man in an alley, you only hurt him. Beat a man with others watching, you hurt his pride." When Little Jed came to settle accounts, only one of us would walk away. I was sure about that.

Knowing I had Taylor behind me with a cocked pistol, I tossed the bloody piece of bottle at the feet of the men that watched. "Anybody else object to US Cavalrymen drinking a beer?" I slid the wolf's skin away from the bar with the toe of my boot.

"Little Jed's no friend of any of us." The bearded man moved back to the bar, grabbed up a glass and held it out to the bartender. "But whoever you are, four wore-out Buffalo Soldiers might not be enough to watch your back. You might need a whole company." He pushed the bills I had laid on the bar my way. "I'll pay for their beer."

My knees went weak, but I flexed the muscles in my legs to keep from shaking.

The bartender shook his head. "Little Jed's like a schoolboy pullin' the legs off'n a hop-toad one at a time, just to see it squirm. Hell only knows what evil he's plottin' right now. You shoulda killed him." The men at the bar nodded. "And that's only the half of it. His daddy makes Little Jed look tame. You heard of a man called Jedidiah Bethea?"

I shook my head.

"Rustler, horse thief, scalp hunter, you name it. Rides with a pack of cutthroats along the border. Word has it he's tradin' repeatin' rifles for Apache gold." The bartender scooped up the money on the bar and filled our mugs. "This is the meanest patch of land God put on a map. Apaches runnin' wild, wolves prowlin' the alleys behind decent folks' homes. Now, Mister Newspaper Man, you've got Little Jed Bethea and his daddy to worry about."

The evening sun sent long rays down the streets of Vengeance. Shopkeepers locked their doors and miners headed for the saloons. The word "Apache" or "wolf" sprinkled every conversation I heard. My eyes searched for a hatchet-faced man with braided hair, but Little Jed Bethea was not to be seen.

By day's end, the town council had paid bounty on two other wolves and listened to a farmer yammer about a drunk cowboy taking a shot at his yard dog. Saunders turned away more customers at his hotel. Every room was full, and the halls, too. He turned his back when I walked past the doors to the Vengeance House.

Then June stepped out of the crowd. A yellow dress as pale as her hair touched the ground around her bare feet. The new shoes I'd bought her dangled from her hand. When she saw me, she skipped down the street and caught my arm.

"Doctor's wife gave me this dress to wear." She stepped back and half-curtsied. Her fingers touched her shiny cheeks. "She brought me hot water for a bath and helped me wash and comb my hair. I ain't felt this clean since the day we left Brokeheart."

"June, there's something else." I touched her hair. "A man brought a string of horses to town. One of them was Seer."

She wrapped her arms around my neck and whispered, "It's a grand day, Kepler. Sergeant Pope gettin' better and all. Me with a new dress. And gettin' Seer back."

I refused to let the easy smile on my face fade away. But I thought of Apaches and wolves and Little Jed Bethea. And though I never said it out loud, I knew I loved this woman. And how wrong I'd been to bring her here.

Chapter Eleven

Teased by the breeze, the lace curtains on the bedroom's windows moved in the first steps of a slow dance. Slanted light from the full moon sliced through the night. June's face rested in the hollow of my shoulder, and my fingers traced from the sun-rough skin on the back of her neck to the cool, smooth places along her spine. Her mouth moved to my throat, and she teased my collarbone with her teeth.

Her softness tightened. She bolted upright. "Someone's watchin' us."

Moonlight flashed on gunmetal. My arm wrapped around her waist, and we tumbled off the bed onto the floor.

A lightning bolt of brightness filled the room. Its own clap of thunder echoed from the walls. A pattern of buckshot raked the bed. Pillow feathers filled the air.

"Stay down." I pulled the riddled blankets from the bed, draped them over June's naked body, and lunged for the door.

"No," she called after me.

Our clothes lay on the parlor floor. I fumbled for my pistol, jerked into my pants, and peered out the front door. The sounds of running boots slapped the dirt between Thomas's house and the corrals behind. Fum's horse bellowed in fright. It dashed along the fence, searching for a way to escape the corral.

I stepped out the door. More footfalls thudded in the dirt alongside the house. I whirled toward the sound and thrust out the pistol to arm's length.

"Don't shoot." Wide eyes stared from the dark. "It's me, Taylor."

I dropped my arm. "I could've killed you."

"I heard the shot. Miss June? Is she . . ."

"She's all right." The horse nickered. A shape slipped through the shadows from the corral to the barn. "Taylor?"

"I see him." He lifted his carbine. "Little Jed?"

"Yeah. Stay with June."

"Take this, suh." He pushed his Springfield into my hands. "That was shotgun I heard."

I tucked my pistol into my waistband, eased back the hammer on Taylor's rifle, and fixed my eyes on the building by the corral. "Don't let anything happen to her." Taylor's Colt was already in his hand.

With the rifle's butt pressed to my shoulder, I kept my face away from the stock so I could see through the night. My bare toes searched the dirt in front of me for my next step. I wanted Little Jed to be waiting. I wanted to end what I'd left undone in the barroom.

Fence rails blended into inky lines. Clouds scraped across the full moon, changing and redrawing each grain of darkness. Behind the shack, where desert brush met the yard, a twig snapped. A stray moonbeam touched a sliver of purple.

Fum's horse rose onto its hind legs. It tossed itself against the rail fence. Wood splintered. The horse heaved itself over the shattered fence and galloped toward the neighboring houses.

Bounding out of the night, a gray wolf took shape. My face clamped to the rifle's stock, but my finger froze, forbidding me to pull the trigger. The wolf's feet touched the ground, and in its next motion it lunged for the barn.

From behind the building the outline of a man stumbled into the moonlight. Braided hair flowed from his silhouette. The wolf caught him in full stride, a gun flew from his hands, and the man slammed into the corral's gate. His arms battled the attacker, trying to pry the wolf's jaws from his throat.

Growls and shrieks and sounds that torture the damned in hell turned my insides icy hot.

In a second it was over.

In the center of the corral, the wolf perched on the man's lifeless chest. The beast twisted its face to the moon and snapped at some morsel that still clung to its mouth. Then, like a wisp of smoke, the animal blended into the grays of the desert night.

Lanterns came to life in the houses around Thomas's. Taylor ran to where I stood rooted to the ground.

"Almighty God."

I searched the darkness for the beast.

"A wolf killed that man." Disbelief filled the soldier's voice.

"Get a torch. Something so we can see." With the rifle still at my shoulder, I edged forward.

Taylor snatched a lantern from a neighbor and told the man to stay where he was. But he followed Taylor to the corral. A Winchester stood at the ready in his hands.

In the circle of yellow light from the lantern,

the gory story was plain. Blood puddled on the ground. Wet splotches dripped from the corral slats. Slick, shiny pieces of the man's entrails lay like long filthy ropes in the dirt. The face was destroyed save for a flap of skin marked with a puckered scar above the dead man's right eye. The neighbor man doubled over and gagged.

"Almighty God," Taylor whispered again.

Chapter Twelve

The sun peeked over the eastern mountains that rimmed Vengeance. The bearded man, who'd brought the wolf hide into the saloon, swung up onto his horse. He rested his rifle across his saddle and studied the ground around his horse's feet. He nodded, and two riders followed him out into the desert behind Thomas's house.

Thomas sat on the back steps and watched them ride away. He filled a coffee mug from the whiskey bottle that sat between us and then held the bottle over my cup. I shook my head.

Taylor led Fum's horse by the halter. A barrel-chested man with a tin star pinned to his shirt walked beside him.

The lawman stopped, peeled off his hat, and wiped his face with a dirty kerchief. "Those wolfers are gonna follow the tracks and see what they can find. They're good at what they do, but somethin' about this tells me they ain't gonna catch up with this wolf." He looked my way, waiting for me to speak. When I didn't, he jammed his hat back on his head. "I never thought I'd feel sorry when I got the word that Little Jed was dead. But no man, not even a snake like him, deserves what he got. Took the undertaker near an hour to pick up all the pieces."

Thomas held up the bottle.

The marshal raised his palm. "No, not now. But I 'spect I'll need some before I shut my eyes tonight." He rested the toe of his boot on the step beside where I sat. "If I was you, I'd think of gettin' out of Vengeance and maybe all of Arizona. When Jedidiah Bethea gets wind that his boy is dead, he'll make someone pay even if it was a wolf that killed him. He hears you cut Little Jed with a bottle in a bar fight . . ." He shook his head. "You might want to ponder on what's worse. Jed Bethea or the Apaches." The lawman tipped his hat. "Officially I'm gonna say death was caused by a wild animal. I'd appreciate if your paper doesn't say any more than that. Folks here have enough to worry about."

"You have my word." Thomas looked into his whiskey. The marshal walked off.

We sat there for a long minute and no one spoke. Thomas lifted his cup. Over the rim, his eyes watched the desert behind his corral. Taylor rocked on his boot heels. June, still wrapped in the torn blankets, stepped out of the house and leaned against the door frame.

Thomas set his cup on the boards beside him but kept his fingers wrapped in the mug's handle. "Remember last year in Leadville? The morning after you left they found the bodies of the two men who were gunnin' for you by the river." He nodded his head toward the corral and barn. "They'd been torn to shreds by wolves." He filled his coffee mug to the rim with whiskey. "You hinted at something that morning, but never really spelled it out. That's why I sent you those newspaper clippin's on the wolves running with the Apaches. Thought it'd bring you here."

I reached out and rested my hand on June's leg. Her warmth, that I had held so close just hours before, had turned icy and she trembled at my touch.

Something down inside prompted me, and words that I had never spoken spilled out. "You should all hear this.

It started my first day in Brokeheart." I poured whiskey into my cup and began the story. "A drunk had been killed. Wolves tore up the body before it was found. At least that was what everyone believed . . ."

As I finished my story, the sun burned down from straight overhead and the bottle was emptied. "Just to toy with me, Landry killed a child in Brokeheart." When my eyes shut I could see it all again. "We trapped her and the wolfman, Nicolae, in their lodge at midnight and set it afire. I saw the flames take hold of him and heard his screams turn to the wails of an animal. When morning came I walked through the ashes. Not a sign, not a sliver of bone. I told myself it was over. And I made myself forget." I looked up from the spot of dirt between my feet. "Men can't change into wolves. Then I got the clippings you sent."

I turned to June for the first time since I had begun. "That picture of the woman. It was Landry. I'm sure of it. And I saw those same eyes in the wolf that tore Little Jed to pieces. I know I did."

June's fingers touched my shoulder. "I trust you, Kep." Tears trailed her cheeks. "You'll do what's right."

I caught her hand in mine and pulled her down until I could wrap her in my arms. "I'll take care of you," I whispered. Her head rested on my shoulder. "I need to write a story for the paper. People only need to know that Little Jed was killed by a wolf." I pulled in a breath and forced the next words through my doubt. "And we'll keep all the rest of what happened here a secret, like the marshal asked."

Thomas nodded. Taylor did the same.

June's tears ran down my chest.

An army of spider feet scurried up my spine. Landry had left a message for me in the corral behind Thomas's house. Why else would she save me from Little Jed's next shotgun blast?

———————

I scribbled out the story about Little Jed on a scrap of paper I found in the parlor room at Thomas's house. When Fum came to check on his horse, I paid him a nickel to drop the page with Thomas at the paper. June made breakfast, but we both only stared at our plates.

She held my arm tighter than I could ever remember when I walked with her to Main Street. I left her at the doctor's and went to the newspaper. A note on my desk told me to meet Thomas at the marshal's office.

Chapter Thirteen

Mesquite smoke tinged the air in the shadowy office. The marshal took a blue-splattered coffeepot from the stove top and filled four tin cups. "This here's Orville Powers. Pinkerton detective workin' out of Tombstone. Does work for the mines."

"Gun work?" I sat on a wood stool at the end of the sheriff's desk and picked up a coffee cup.

Powers had taken a chair at the other end of the desk.

"If need be." He took a black hat from his head and placed it on the desk. Like his black coat and pants, there wasn't a speck of dust on the Stetson. His hair was silver and laid close to his head. The outline of a Remington derringer pressed against his vest pocket, and the ivory butt of a nickel-plated Colt hung under his arm in a huckleberry shoulder rig. Like the band on his hat, the holster was made of rattlesnake hide.

He tapped his fingers on a copy of *The Vengeance Dispatch* that lay on the desk. "I read your story about the stagecoach attack. Good writing."

Thomas straddled a chair next to me. "I don't think you two called us here to talk about a newspaper."

The sheriff put one foot on an empty gunpowder keg. He leaned over his desk and spread out a map. "Show us where the Apaches jumped your stage."

I found Vengeance on the map, traced the stage route north with my thumbnail, and tapped the paper.

"You're sure, now?" the sheriff asked.

"As sure as I can be."

The sheriff marked the spot I pointed to with the lead tip of a bullet. "Dupree's place is about here." He moved less than an inch on the map and made another "x", and then looked at Powers. "See there, that's what I told you."

Powers cleared his throat. He paused like a stage actor waiting for the curtain to rise and then began to talk. "All the reports about this Apache war party have them south of here. Crook put three companies of cavalry in the field. He wants to cut them off before they reach the reservations and rile up a passel of young warriors to join up with them." Powers picked at a piece of lint that had settled on his coat. "This bunch to the north must be a different band."

The marshal made some marks on his map south of Vengeance.

"Tell 'em what you told me 'bout Bethea. Kepler ought to know."

Powers raised a finger to his nose as if to stifle a sneeze. I thought it was a gesture to hold his audience's attention.

Finally he spoke. "Jedidiah Bethea has twenty men with him. He took delivery of fifty new Winchesters in Lordsburg. The Pinkerton man there sent word Bethea and his men were seen riding west."

The lawman made a mark at Lordsburg and drew an arrow pointing west. "See there. Indians to the north and south. Cavalry at least three days away. Outlaws ridin' west. And right in the middle"—he drew a circle on the map—"a town called Vengeance."

A fist pounded on the closed door. "Marshal, you better get out here," a man called. "You need to see this."

We followed him out the door. A man leading a lathered horse stood in the middle of the street. A body sprawled across its saddle.

"It's one of those wolfers," the man said.

"Where'd you find him?"

"Not even a mile from town."

"There was three of them," the sheriff barked back.

"There was. Nothing left but pieces of the other two."

"Apaches?"

"No, sir. I think wolves got 'em."

I made an addition to the map in my mind. Apaches north and south. Bethea coming from the east. And wolves a mile from town.

"Heaven help us," the marshal whispered.

———————

The marshal went off with the dead wolfer's body. Thomas turned to Powers. "What you didn't tell us was why you're here in Vengeance."

The Pinkerton man smoothed the front of his coat. I could tell his habit was never to answer a question quickly. He strummed the vest pocket over his derringer and finally spoke. "Came in this morning from Tombstone. Rode guard on the mine's payroll. Outlaws and Apaches about, we took extra precautions." Powers looked over Thomas's shoulder at me. "Headed back in the morning with three wagons of equipment. Keep this secret now, but the mine superintendent is having us take his wife and daughter along. Two other managers are sending their women. I'll be gone first thing in the morning."

Powers tipped his Stetson and walked away, down Main Street to the saloons and brothels.

As Thomas and I walked to the newspaper office, even the noise on the street seemed quiet. Two storekeepers passed by. Their coat pockets bulged with the bulk of revolvers. Miners, teamsters, and cowhands kept their rifles close. There were whispers as I passed. Muted words about Little Jed and a wolf.

Everyone kept an eye toward the desert. Watching for what might come. Apaches or outlaws.

I watched for wolves.

The four troopers lolled around a campfire they had built in the yard in front of Thomas's house. The coals glowed as red as the last thread of the sunset sky. June jumped from her spot by the fire when she saw me. Her arms wrapped tight around a bundle. She stumbled over to greet me.

"It's a puppy, Kep. Nothin' but a yellow cur dog. Its momma whelped it out under a shed near the doctor's house. Can I keep it? Won't be no trouble."

The pup's shiny black nose peeked out from the scrap of blanket June had wrapped it in. Its pink tongue lashed June's chin. The melody of her laughter followed.

I tried to hold a stern look. "You give it a name?"

"If'n you let me keep him"—she dangled the dog by his shoulders so I could see it was a male—"I'm gonna call him Trooper. On account of Taylor and the sergeant and the others."

A smile won over my pretended sternness. I rubbed Trooper's ear. "You like animals, don't you, June?"

"Sometimes more than people." A frown washed her smile away. "'Member back in Brokeheart when that fancy lady killed my cat?"

I scooped Trooper from June's arm. I wrapped my free arm around June's shoulders and rested my chin on the top of her head. "She won't hurt you ever again."

Fresh lumber covered the bedroom window Little Jed had blasted away.

"You boys do that?" I nodded at the window.

"Yes, suh. Thomas bought the boards and told us where he kept his tools." Taylor stood and dusted off the seat of his pants.

"Good work." The puppy struggled in my arms. I stroked its nose. "Any word from the fort?"

"We 'posed to sit tight until the troops that are following the Apaches come this way." Taylor tossed another log on the fire. "We'll stay and guard the house tonight."

"No, go on. Get some rest."

"But, suh—"

"We'll be safe tonight."

The soldiers dipped their heads to June, gathered their rifles, and headed for town. I refused to move my arm from her shoulders. With the heat from the fire touching our faces, we watched the sunset paint the heavens.

A cotton-top quail set its wings and soared across the evening sky. It lit on a fence rail at the back corral. Trooper fought my arms, and a quiet low rumble vibrated in his chest. The quail key-awed, and a dozen more answered back. One by one they soared in to join the first.

"Peaceful tonight, Kepler." June slipped her arms around my waist and let Trooper slurp her face. "Seems like everything 'bout last night didn't never happen. It's right when simple good makes you forget the bad."

————————

June boiled up water and brewed tea from a tin she found in Thomas's cupboards. She poured the tea into china cups painted with red roses and held her little finger out straight when she sipped it. The pup found a warm spot on the kitchen floor and fell asleep. June giggled at the pup's snores and her straight finger. She did a curtsy and danced on her tiptoes into the parlor.

Maybe I could live in a house like this one. Perhaps I could trade rented rooms for something I owned. Something with a fence, a dog, and even a rocking chair. A place to share with the woman I so wanted to protect.

I opened the door to cool the house. What was left of the moon glazed the sky like frost might paint an autumn morning. Specks of light sparkled from each sage branch, each cactus spine, and even the grains of sand showed the magic.

Trooper heard me. He stretched and ambled out onto the porch steps beside me. The same rumble he made when he saw the quail quivered in the little dog's chest. He scratched at the floorboards, and his tail stopped its wag.

By the fence, where there had been nothing before, a shadow stirred. I pushed the puppy back into the house with my boot and shut the door. My fingers dug behind my hip for Mother's pistol. I eased the hammer to full cock and pressed my back flat against the house, trying to make myself into a shade of the dark.

Night birds and crickets hushed. The thump of my pulse threatened to betray me.

Where Little Jed had died last night, the shadow swirled again. A twist in the dark became a shoulder. Moonlight sketched the flow of a skirt. Hands brushed back a scarf. Through the last smoke of the soldiers' dying campfire, the slightest shade of purple gleamed from a woman's eyes.

Night and dark fell away, and I saw her plainly. Landry gathered her skirts, knelt, and grazed the bloodstained dirt with her fingers. Her purple-tinged eyes found me, and she touched a fingertip to her tongue.

"Kepler." My name floated on the moonlight, and like the wisp of smoke that carried Little Jed's killer away, she was gone.

My knees fought to hold me up. Night shadows menaced, and I pointed my pistol at every one.

I backed through the door into the house and slammed it behind me.

"Kepler? What is it?" June had the dog in her arms.

Once before, when I had my chance to flee this demon, I had stayed. The ripples of that decision led me to Vengeance. All the promises I had made to June raced through my mind. My teeth bit down on my lip until blood came.

"Get your things together. There'll be wagons in the morning. We're leaving Vengeance."

Somewhere on the desert, but as close as the locked door, a wolf howled.

Chapter Fourteen

With my pistol in my fist and the silver bullet under the cocked hammer, I peered out at the changing shadows around the corral posts. Through the night, I questioned whether it was Landry that taunted me or just something my mind had conjured up. Just before dawn, June's steady breathing blended with the sound of the pup's. But sleep never found me. Even as sunrise washed the darkness away, I wrestled with doubts as to what I'd really seen.

A need to find some proof pushed away caution. I stalked out to the corral with the pistol in my hand. I saw marks from where a woman's skirts had brushed the surface of the stained sand. Pressed into the soil, behind those marks, were a pair of tracks. Not from a woman's shoes but the tracks of a wolf. The hind feet. From a she-wolf that walked on two legs.

June stood in the house's front doorway. The puppy tugged on her skirt tail.

I lowered the pistol's hammer and walked back to the house. "We need to go."

"Tell me there'll be another house. A place like this we can live in." Her hands clutched her stomach and I thought she was going to be sick.

"Someday, June. Someday we'll have a fine house.

Bigger than this one. You can have a yard full of puppies. But now I need to take you where you can be safe."

Tears streaked her cheeks. "I put the new things you bought me in a flour sack. Let me get them."

———————

The stable boy led my sorrel horse from the barn. "That'll be another ten dollars for the saddle, Mister Kepler." The mop-headed kid rubbed Seer's muzzle. "The old man that owns this place is mighty proud of those wore ole saddles he's got around here. I was you, I'd go buy somewhere else. There's two or three places on Main that will sell you a new one for a dollar more."

"Don't have time. You find a set of saddlebags to go with it?"

"I can. He'll want another dollar for 'em."

I flipped a silver dollar his way. "Go get 'em."

The kid plucked it out of the air. "Yes, sir." He rubbed the coin on his pants. "I gonna miss that horse of yours. Just last night, Seer there put up a ruckus. I was sleeping in the loft and when I looked out back, a big ole wolf was prowlin' the edge of the corrals. It ran off when I lit a torch. With all that's been happenin' 'round here it made my skin crawl. Reckon it mighta been the wolf that killed Little Jed?"

June dug her fingers into my arm. I looked down into her eyes. She shook her head and I shrugged my shoulders.

"Smitty, they're supposed to be some wagons leaving town this morning. You know anything about that?"

"Yes, sir." He held out Seer's reins.

June shifted the puppy onto her hip. Seer swung his face close and nuzzled the dog. June's mouth turned up in a smile.

"Most horses shy away from dogs. Even a pup like that one." Smitty let tobacco juice dribble from the corner of his mouth. "I'm hopin' someday I can have a horse like Seer."

"The wagons?"

"That man that dresses in black—"

"Powers?"

"Yeah, him. Had 'em load up three wagons last night over to the mine company's warehouse. Heard they're leavin' at noon."

"That seems a late start for Tombstone."

"Didn't hear nothin' said 'bout Tombstone. But that Powers"—Smitty shook his head—"he's a strange one. Let me get those saddlebags."

June wanted to see Sergeant Pope before we left town. I walked her to the doctor's and told her I'd be back for her after I talked with Thomas.

———————

A half-full whiskey glass sat on the corner of Thomas's desk. The bottle beside it was nearly empty. "You're doin' the right thing, Kepler." He twirled the glass with his fingers but never lifted it. "Wish I'd been man enough to take my wife and boy and leave this town." He looked out the window. A tear welled in the corner of his eye.

"When we get to Tombstone, I'll put June on a train back to Colorado. I'll get back here as soon as I can."

"Don't come back. You take that girl and run as far as you can from this place." Thomas leaned forward over his desk. His elbow brushed his glass and it shattered on the floor. He caught my shirtsleeve and pulled until he lifted out of his chair. "Don't come back here, hear me?"

My mind saw Landry kneeling in the corral and I heard

my name float through the air. "Maybe I'm the only one that can end this."

Thomas sagged into his chair. He lifted the bottle to his lips as I left.

———————

Powers's black Stetson shined like a crow's wing in the noonday sun. He barked orders to the teamster boys. I wrapped Seer's reins around a corral post. June held her dog on her hip, I took her by the hand, and we walked to the wagons.

"Powers," I called out.

Sweat rings circled his armpits, and his white shirt clung to a wet streak down the center of his back. He turned when he heard me and jumped down from the wagon.

"Kepler, what are you doing here?" Powers looked at June beside me and touched the brim of his hat.

"We want to go with you to Tombstone. I'll pay what you ask."

He pushed his hat back, fished a kerchief from his back pocket, and mopped his face. He tipped his head toward June. "Who's this?"

"She's with me."

June hugged the pup tight over her chest as Powers let his eyes sweep over her.

I tugged on her hand and she stepped behind me. "How much?"

Powers dabbed his forehead again and then shook out the kerchief. Like a man choosing a good horse, his eyes never left June.

"Powers, I said I'll pay."

"Could use another gun. Your lady and the dog ride in

a wagon. You ride with me, up at the front." He turned and cursed at the boys harnessing the mules. "Smitty," he hollered. "Help these folks stow their gear."

The blond kid from the stable sauntered over. "Mister Kepler." He nodded his head and picked up June's sack of clothes. "This all you got?" He scratched Trooper's nose.

"What are you doing here?"

Smitty dribbled tobacco juice on the ground. "That old man that owns the stable chewed my backside somethin' fierce for sellin' you those saddlebags for a dollar." He wiped his lips. "I told him he could kiss me where he left his tooth marks and walked off. Came over here and hired on. With all the talk of Apaches and outlaws, I thought a smart man might want to leave Vengeance."

Smitty glanced over his shoulder at Powers. The Pinkerton man checked the mules' harnesses.

The boy let his voice drop. "Somethin' ain't right about the covered wagon. I'll show you what I mean when he's not looking." Smitty caught the next trickle of tobacco juice with the back of his hand. "Know somethin' else? 'Sides me and those Mexican kids, he's only got an old man for a driver." Smitty shook his head. "This was my outfit, I'd want as many men with rifles as I could find." He spit on the ground. "Glad you're comin' along, Mister Kepler. Glad you're comin' along."

I could feel the hairs on the back of my neck pull away from the sweat on my skin and stand on end. June's fingers slipped from my hand. She staggered a step, and Trooper dropped from her grasp. I caught her by the waist.

"June?"

The color had washed from her face. Marks as dark as bruises formed half circles under her eyes.

"June?"

"I'm so hot." She leaned heavy in my arm.

I pulled her tight, found her legs with my other arm, and lifted her from the ground. She weighed no more than the flour sack she carried her dresses in.

I carried her to the shade of the warehouse building and set her on a wooden crate. Trooper nosed at June's skirt. My fingers pushed strands of her white-blond hair from her eyes. "Are you all right?" Then, over my shoulder, I said, "Smitty, get some water."

June mashed her eyes shut and slowly shook her head. "No," she said, "no. Ahh, I feel—"

Smitty brought a dog-skin water bag and held it out for June. June gulped at the liquid.

"Easy. Just sip it." I touched her face.

She pushed my hands away and rubbed wet fingers over her cheeks. "I feel better now."

"We can wait and take the next stage to Tombstone."

"No, Kepler. I want to leave this town." She lifted her dog and rubbed her face along his back.

A shadow moved across the dirt next to where I knelt. Powers stooped down beside me. "What's happenin' here?"

"Heat got to her," I said.

Powers reached out and put his hand on June's leg. A low growl rumbled up in Trooper's chest.

June pushed his hand away. "I said I'm fine now." She straightened her back and set her jaw.

Powers stood. "It won't get no cooler. Get her somethin' to put on her head and have her drink plenty of water. We'll be leavin' here shortly." He touched her leg again. Even in the heat, a shiver coursed through her. Then Powers let his fingers trail across her skirt.

I caught his wrist and squeezed until I could feel bone.

Powers wrestled his arm free, stood, and tipped his hat. "Drink plenty of water, little lady. It's gonna be a hot one." He ambled off to the wagons.

Rage bubbled up inside me. But June collected the drops that seeped through the canvas bag with her palm and wiped it across her throat. She watched Powers walk away, and the muscles along her jaw tightened.

"We're not going. I won't let him paw at you like a common—" The word I didn't say echoed empty in my head.

"Never mind him. I had worse done to me in Brokeheart."

I always thought I was a strong man. That I faced decisions with a cool head. Those traits have served me well around a poker table and the times gunplay was the only answer. I had June to care for. Pride be damned. The choices I made needed to be for the both of us.

The Mexican kids who had harnessed the mules came close and peered at June. I tapped the brim of one's straw hat. "How much?" I dug into my vest pocket for my coins.

The boy smiled. I took two bits from my pocket and held it out.

The boy tugged the hat from his head and snatched the coin from my hand. "*Gracias.*"

I took the sombrero and turned to June. "Wear this when you're out in the sun. Now wait here and rest." Such a small gift for the woman who gave so much.

———

I pulled Seer's reins free from the post and found Powers watching the last bit of freight being loaded into one of the wagons. Seer pulled back and nickered when I approached the Pinkerton man. I grabbed Powers by the shoulder and turned him to face me. "I'll do what you say 'til we get to Tombstone, but you stay clear of June." I leaned in close enough that the whiskers on his face moved with my breath. "You lay a finger on her again, you'll pay hell."

Powers didn't step back. He took the shaft of straw he had been chewing from between his lips and tapped it on his front teeth. His pale eyes never blinked. The fingers of his other hand hooked in the waistband of his pants. I thought of the derringer I knew he carried. My fists balled and muscles coiled.

"You tough, Kepler?" He looked over my shoulder to June in the shady spot. His tongue flicked at the stalk of straw. "They served me a tough beefsteak for supper last night. You know how I handle tough? I cut it up in little pieces and chew it up one piece at a time." Powers turned his back and walked away. "We leave as soon as the next wagon is loaded. I'm not waitin' for you or your lady."

———————

June cradled her pup in one arm and climbed onto the wagon seat beside Smitty. She pushed his hand away when he offered to help. The fingers of one hand clamped on the rope that lashed the crates, and her knuckles turned as white as her face. Trooper snuggled in her lap. She tilted the sombrero on her head so that I could not see her face.

A covered wagon wheeled across the yard. The driver popped his blacksnake whip in the air. He tugged on the reins and snapped the whip again. A step at time, the team of four backed the wagon to the loading dock. A door to the warehouse office swung open, and a woman about June's age with honey-colored hair stepped out.

Powers took her arm, led her to back of the wagon, and helped her climb in. He met another woman at the door. She tucked her dark hair into her bonnet and stuck out her hand. A girl, in a matching dress and hat, took her hand. They followed Powers to the wagon. While they climbed in, Powers returned to the office.

A steely-haired man in a worn suit stepped into the sun. A stout woman, with hair as gray as the man's, came onto the dock. She shook her head. The man placed his arm over her shoulder and walked her to the wagon. She held tight to his hand as he coaxed her to get in.

Powers moved in and pulled their hands apart. He shoved the man back and pushed her into the wagon with the others. He called to the driver, a whip snapped, and the team strained at its harness. The woman's arm waved from the opening in the canvas. Over the noise of the wagons and mules, the last woman's sobs hung in the hot dust-filled air.

Powers climbed onto a pinto gelding. He waved and the covered wagon followed him out of the yard onto a dirt road that led out of town. Smitty pulled his freight wagon in behind. In the swirl of dust, the third wagon followed. The three Mexican boys perched on its seat. The one who had sold me his hat held the reins. Smoke from the chimneys at the mine's smelter flavored the grit in the air.

I swung onto Seer's saddle and rode up beside Smitty. He spit a wad of tobacco to the ground beside the moving wagon. The spray of brown juice speckled his face.

"Mister Kepler"—he popped the rein ends on the mules' rumps—"if we're headed for Tombstone, it appears

Powers is taking the long way around. We should be takin' that other road."

"Kepler," Powers hollered back. "Ride up with me."

I pulled up, let the wagons pass, and then spurred Seer to June's side of the wagon. "It's not too late," I called to her. "We can stay."

"No, Kepler. I want to go far from this place. Where that wolf won't ever find us."

My stomach turned sour. "Then we'll go." I touched my heels to Seer's sides and rode up to Powers.

We passed the last buildings on the outskirts of Vengeance.

"Shouldn't we take the other road? It's the shorter way to Tombstone, am I right?"

Powers kicked his horse's ribs. I clucked to Seer to keep the pace.

"Did you hear me?"

Powers plucked the shaft of straw from his lips and let the hot wind carry it away. "I heard you. I'm in charge here and we'll take the road I choose. And keep your voice down." He glanced back at the wagons behind us. "Word on the street is that these three wagons have equipment for one of the mines down the valley some. Only you, the sheriff, and the superintendent at the mine know about Tombstone."

Powers pulled up on his horse and waited for the wagons. "The women in the wagon—superintendent's wife and daughter, the others are wives of two of his managers I told you about. All the talk about Apaches, they wanted to get their women out of Vengeance." He stroked his horse's neck while the wagons caught up to us. "I told 'em to sit tight in the back of the wagon so as not to get noticed. That fat old one might have spoiled all that with her cryin' and carryin' on. Never can be too sure who's watching." He scanned the ridgeline.

When the wagons came closer, Powers nudged his horse onto the trail. "There'll be a junction in two, three hours. We'll take a steep trail up the canyon, camp on top, and be in Tombstone before nightfall tomorrow. I'm bankin' that the cavalry'll be between us and the Apaches." Powers looked at me. "And that Bethea will be ridin' hard to find you in Vengeance. You did right to get out of there."

"What if you guessed wrong about the Apaches? And Bethea?"

Powers turned his horse into the trail. "There's an extra rifle in the third wagon. Have one of them boys give it to you." He pointed down at the trail. Wolf tracks marked the dust. "And Kepler, watch for wolves."

Chapter Fifteen

Faint ruts in the hard-baked soil marked the trail that split from the main road. The mules dropped their heads lower and strained into the harness. Steel-rimmed wheels pulverized the crusty dirt. Clouds of dust, as fine as sifted flour, welled up around the animals' feet and clung to the strings of slobber that trailed from the mules' mouths.

The wagons labored up the mountainside, lurching over rocks and pounding through sagebrush grown up in the trail. June slumped forward on the wagon seat. Smitty's arm shot out to steady her, and he pulled up on his team. "Whoa, there."

The Mexican boy jerked his wagon to a stop behind them.

"Powers, we need rest. The stock needs water." I wheeled Seer around and headed for the wagon with June.

Powers raised his hand to signal the driver of the lead wagon. "Ease up, Swede." He swung down from his saddle. "We'll stop here. Water your teams."

I jumped down from Seer, reached up, and lifted June from the wagon seat. Her legs failed her and she sank into a shady spot against the wagon wheel. She clutched her hands around her middle. Trooper nosed at June's face.

I took my canteen from the saddle. "Just a few sips now." I pulled the stopper and held it out to her.

"I don't know what happened. My legs just wouldn't

hold me." June brought the water to her mouth and drank. Droplets spilled down her chin. Trooper nosed at June's face and lapped at the stray drops. A smile curled the corner of her lips. "I feel better."

"You rest there." Inside, I cursed myself for bringing her here. Not just here, but to chase wolfmen in Arizona. I touched her face.

Smitty stepped close. "Mister Kepler." He looked at Powers. "Help me water the mules," he said loudly. He tipped his head toward the wagon bed.

June poured water into her palm for the dog. Trooper slurped it up. "Go on, I'm all right now," she told me.

I followed Smitty to water kegs lashed to the back of the wagon.

He splashed the pail into the barrel. "Somethin' ain't right." He held out the pail for me to take. "When you can, look at that covered wagon. Shouldn't ride that low with nothin' but those womenfolk in the back."

I took the pail of water to the mules while Smitty filled another. While the animals drank, I eyed the wagon. The leaf springs behind the wheel where June rested strained at the load. A quick look at the covered wagon showed the same.

Smitty moved up with a bucket for the other mules. "See what I mean?"

I nodded. "What you think?"

"Can't be sure," he muttered. "I gonna take a close look when we stop for the night. Whatever Powers hid in them crates is heavier than I thought it was. That's for sure." He mopped the sweat from his face with his free hand.

"There's nothing in that wagon except three women

and a girl." I stepped close to him as I moved the pail to the next mule.

"I ain't figured that out yet." He hocked his chew at the mules' feet.

The canvas on the covered wagon rippled as one of the women pulled herself out of the back and climbed to the ground. The girl caught the woman's hands and swung to the ground. The older woman brushed the dust from the girl's dress before she swept her hands over her own.

Powers strode to the woman and spoke. She bristled at his words, crossed her arms across her chest, and shook her head. She took the girl's hand and walked to where June sat. Powers tilted back his Stetson and jabbed his hands into his pants pockets.

"Miss," the woman said to June, "I'm Miriam Hawes. This is my daughter Josie. We can see you're feeling poorly and we want you to ride in the covered wagon with the rest of us. It won't be any cooler, but you'll be out of the sun. The driver is a vile man. Every other word is an oath to the Almighty, but it's better than you riding out here in this awful sun."

The girl knelt. "May I pet your dog?"

June held out the pup and the freckles on her nose wrinkled. "His name's Trooper."

Josie touched the top of Trooper's head, and his tongue licked at her fingers.

June looked up at Miriam Hawes. "What will Mister Powers say?"

"What Mister Powers thinks does not concern me. My husband is the mine's superintendent, and Mister Powers works for him." She held out her hand to help June stand.

"Come along, Josie. And bring the puppy." She turned to me. "Mister Kepler, isn't it?"

"Yes, Ma'am. And thank you."

"I am a Christian woman, Mister Kepler. I'm doing what I believe is right." She patted her daughter on the shoulder as the girl walked by, and Miriam Hawes moved a half step closer to me. "I've read the things you wrote in the paper. You have a way with words." She glanced to where Powers stood at the covered wagon. "And I am glad you're here, Mister Kepler. I don't like the way Powers looks at my daughter. I don't trust the man."

I handed Trooper to Josie as soon she was in the wagon. Then I took June by the hips and lifted her in.

"Gladys Jean, this is Mister Kepler. He writes for the newspaper in Vengeance. I'm sure you've read his work. June is his"—Miriam Hawes paused—"friend. She'll be sharing the covered wagon with us."

The gray-haired woman turned her face. Her arms looked like sausage meat straining at their casings. She huffed out a word I couldn't understand.

"Veronica," Miriam said to the third woman, "say hello to June." Dirt streaked Veronica's face and clung to the fine hair on her upper lip. Golden curls strayed from her bonnet, but there was a smile on her face. I guessed her age to be no more than twenty.

June settled onto the wagon floor. I reached to take Miriam's hand. "Miss Hawes, did your husband say anything about the equipment in these wagons?"

"We never talk of his business."

I eyed the back of the wagon looking for a clue of what could make it so heavy.

Miriam took my hand and stepped up. "Mister Kepler." She peered around the wagon to look at Powers. "My father owned a freight company. I've been around teams and wagons my entire life." She let go of my hand. "I've had the same thoughts."

"Time to get movin'" Powers shouted. "We've got a ways to go before we camp for the night."

The trail flattened near the top of the mountain. Steep rock walls on both sides shaded a place just wide enough for a practiced teamster to turn a team of four and wagon full around, but no more. Rounded slabs of pink stone littered the canyon floor like poker chips on a great table. Shadows cast by the canyon's walls cooled the day's heat.

Powers called for us to stop. "We'll make camp here."

"We got more than another hour of daylight." I tipped back the brim of my hat so I could study the rim of the canyon.

"It'll be cool for the women. We can build up a fire and the walls will hide the light."

"Apaches sneak up on top of the canyon walls, it'll be like shooting fish in a barrel," I told him. "I don't like it."

"Tell you what, Kepler." He pointed at a damp smear on the rock wall that led to a marshy seep. "You help water the teams. I'll ride up ahead and look for signs. If it looks safe, we'll camp here. If not, we'll make for the top. Either way the stock needs water. We might not find any up ahead." He clucked to his pinto horse and rode off.

Smitty unhitched his team and led them to the

little water hole, and the Mexican kids loosed their mules and waited their turn. The old man that drove the covered wagon pulled out a whiskey bottle he'd kept hidden and sipped at it. He hollered for the Mexicans to care for his team and made no effort to leave his wagon seat.

The women passed a canteen around. Josie wore June's straw hat. She found a stick and tossed it for Trooper to chase. Veronica sat on a rock and June brushed her hair. Gladys Jean fanned her jowls with her bonnet.

Miriam Hawes excused herself and came to where I watered the mules. "Mister Kepler." She patted one of the animals on the back, stroked along its neck with her fingers, and turned her back to the wagon driver. "I've been studying the wagon while we rode along. I believe someone has built a false floor in it. Whoever did was quite skilled." She scratched the mule's ear. "I think there's something hidden in the wagon."

I lifted the mule's head from the swampy water. "That would account for why the wagon appears so heavy."

"What could it be?"

The tip of my tongue drew a circle on the inside of my cheek. "Your husband's a miner. A gold miner."

Her voice went cold. "I heard him and the other managers. With all this talk of Apaches and outlaws there was concern. Then this Pinkerton man, Powers, shows up from headquarters." Her forehead touched the mule's back. "They've hidden gold in the wagons. They're not taking any chances. The want to get the gold to Tombstone where it will be safe."

"If that's so, there's nothing we can do about it."

"I don't trust Powers one bit."

I touched the pistol in my belt. "He's done nothing to make us *not* trust him."

"If word slipped out about the gold, we could be in danger. Secrets are hard to keep in Vengeance."

"Don't say a word to the others. We'll be in Tombstone sometime tomorrow."

Just then, Powers rode his horse back to the wagons. "You boys build up a cook fire. We're spending the night here." He took the whiskey bottle from the Swede and tilted the bottom to the sky. When he watched June pull the brush through Veronica's hair, his tongue touched his lips.

I looked at the rim of the canyon walls above us. "Miss Hawes, you said you were a Christian woman. You might want to say a prayer."

———————

After they watered the mules, Smitty and one of the Mexican boys took the animals down the canyon and picketed them on a strip of grass. The two other boys took bundles of wood from the back of their wagon and got a fire going.

Powers put on his shoulder rig and hung the shiny Colt in its holster. It was the first time he'd carried a gun all day. If there was no trouble up ahead, I wondered why he chose now to find his pistol.

The Swede finished his whiskey and dozed on the wagon seat. He had propped his rifle against the brake handle. The women enjoyed the cool of the valley floor. June, Josie, and Veronica played keep-away with Trooper. Their laughter rang off the rock walls and echoed down the canyon like some distant circus music.

Miriam Hawes took Gladys Jean by the arm and led

the stout woman away from the wagons to a cluster of barrel-sized rocks in the shadow of the canyon walls. The big woman scuffed the toes of her shoes through the dirt and slapped at a swarm of gnats that circled her face.

I took the saddle off Seer's back. His ears stood on end like he was listening for something I could not hear. I slipped the rifle Powers had given me from its scabbard, opened the lever enough to be sure there was a live round under the hammer, and leaned it against Smitty's wagon. With a handful of dry grass, I rubbed Seer's back and legs. All the while, my eyes studied the rocky rim above our little camp.

At the sheriff's office in Vengeance, Powers had told us that Jedidiah Bethea and his men were headed west from Lordsburg with fifty new Winchesters. I tried to remember the map the sheriff had laid on his desk. If I was right, the road we had taken when we left Vengeance led northeast. Then we'd followed the trail up the mountain. It led south. That put us on a line due east of Lordsburg.

Seer's muscles tightened under my fingers. A wolf's howl echoed down the canyon, chasing away the sounds of the women's laughter. I bit down on my tongue.

"What was that?" Gladys Jean bolted up from the rock where she sat. Her hands swatted at her arms. She tugged up on her skirt tail and slapped at her petticoats.

"Just an old coyote." Missus Hawes reached out to touch her, but Gladys Jean pulled away. "Settle yourself. You've heard that sound a thousand times."

Gladys Jean's fingers dug into the folds on her neck. "Ants," she blubbered. "I'm covered with ants." The old woman's flesh shook with her sobs.

An ugly laugh boiled up from deep inside of Powers.

Men exist that enjoy seeing pain. Those that laugh at crippled dogs and find humor at hog slaughter time. Those that take an extra step to mash a sand lizard. Those that taunt a scared old woman. Powers wore a new black Stetson and shiny boots, but grave dirt filled his heart.

Gladys Jean supped in her tears. She tried to make words come, but more noises blubbered out. Missus Hawes put her arm over the old woman's rounded shoulders and they turned their backs to Powers.

Little Josie moved away from June and the dog. She put her hands on her hips and stared at Powers. "You're a mean man, you are." Words I could expect her mother might say shot from the little girl.

Whiskey clouded his eyes as Powers's laugh roiled up again. "How old are you, missy?"

"I'm twelve." She stuck out her chin and refused to step back.

"That's what I thought. 'Bout twelve. That's good."

Powers's laugh slammed into the canyon walls and echoed back a thousand times.

"Josie!" Missus Hawes snatched her daughter's hand and pulled her away. She led Josie and Gladys Jean to the covered wagon.

June scooped Trooper from the ground. In a dozen quick steps she was beside me. She touched my arm, and when I looked in her face, her eyes pleaded. "Look at Seer. He knows somethin'. Kep, bad's comin'."

Seer tossed his head and whinnied. In that second, the heat of the day left the canyon floor and the air turned cold.

Shadows stretched and flowed like liquid down the canyon walls. The pink and red sandstone melted into gray shades and then swirled into oily browns like the skim on old coffee. Spikes sent by the orange sunset showed at the canyon rim, but where we camped, night settled in so quickly I could feel it brush over my skin.

Even the flames from the cook fire lost their battle with the dark. The blaze fought to give heat, and the white light only twisted the shadows more.

The women settled into the covered wagon. I doubted any would sleep well.

I tucked my chin into my collar and settled my back against the wagon. I added together every thought from the day as if I was to compose a story. Overloaded wagons could be gold, or there could be another answer. My only conclusion was agreement with Josie Hawes. Powers was a vile man.

Dawn would come to the canyon top with a splash of new light. Down in this valley, it would creep in like the ants that tortured Gladys Jean.

Chapter Sixteen

The mules stirred at first light. Hooves brushed over the hard-packed dirt. Without lifting my face, I searched the shrinking shadows for movement. Not a cricket chirped. No birds called. Most mornings the quiet was a comfort. Today it settled around me with a strangeness that puckered my guts.

Near the fire, Powers and the Swede watched the canyon's rim, rifles at the ready.

I reached for the Winchester I had leaned against the wagon. Like a rattlesnake strike, hands caught my arm. A forearm pressed across my throat, pinning my head to the wagon.

Dark eyes stared into mine. The tip of a knife touched my throat.

His hand found the pistol tucked behind my hip. He pulled it away and jammed it into the front of his belt. In a blur, his fist shot forward into my stomach. All the air left my lungs.

Smitty tumbled onto the ground in front of me. Blood soaked his blond hair. He fought his way to his knees. A mountain of a man whacked Smitty between his shoulder blades with the butt of his rifle. Somehow the boy kept his feet under him.

"Powers, help me," he gasped out. Blood and tobacco juice dribbled from his mouth.

Powers thumbed back the hammer on his rifle and trained the muzzle on the giant's stomach. His lips turned up in a smile. He swung the rifle to Smitty's chest and pulled the trigger.

The slug tore a hole in Smitty's shirtfront and ripped out a chunk of flesh the size of a hen's egg from his back. The boy's hands trembled but couldn't find their way to the wound in his chest. His eyes asked a question that would never be answered, and he fell onto his face.

"Powers, you bastard—" The fist smashed into my stomach again.

Powers took a bottle of whiskey from the Swede. He pulled the cork with his teeth, took a drink, and held it out. "Jedediah."

I twisted my head enough to see a heavy-chested man walk around the end of the wagon. He stepped over Smitty's body and took the bottle from Powers. Greasy hair drooped from the back of a cast-off cavalryman's cap, and a shiny new Winchester hung in the crook of his elbow.

On the rocks above us, shapes in the dawn light became the silhouettes of other men with rifles.

"'Sides the gold and women I promised, got a special prize for you." Powers pointed his rifle at me. "That fella your Comanche is ticklin' with the point of his knife. That's the newspaperman that caused Little Jed to be killed by the wolf."

Bethea turned and walked to me. I struggled, but the Indian pressed the very tip of the blade of his knife into my Adam's apple.

"Gatlin," Bethea called to his giant. "Find some rope and help Solo tie Mister Kepler to the wagon wheel. I want him to think for a long time about how my boy screamed when that wolf tore him to pieces." He reached over the Indian's shoulder and flicked a fly from the tip of my nose. "With every mile I rode, I been thinkin' of ways to kill you."

A wail filled the air. "No-o-o." June scrambled from the wagon and hurled herself toward me. Bethea's giant caught her with one arm and hoisted her like a rag doll. Other outlaws tore back the canvas and dragged the women onto the ground. Miriam Hawes clawed at her attacker's eyes until she shook free. She pulled Josie from another's grasp and shielded her daughter behind her.

I fought the arms that held me, something inside me needing to go to June. To grab her and take her from this place. The hand that held the knife swung in an arc. The butt of the hilt glanced off my cheekbone, taking skin with it. Fire sliced into my brain, and I fought to keep my eyes open.

Gladys Jean's cries quivered like a hurt piglet. She tried to run, but stumbled. An outlaw pushed her down with the toe of his boot. The ground beneath her skirts puddled wet around her. She tried to crawl away, but her tormentor kicked her and she fell into the mud she had made.

The giant caught Veronica around the neck with his hairy forearm. While June scratched at the side of his face, he bent forward and licked the blond girl's cheek.

"You did well, Powers. Both of those"—he pointed at June and Veronica in the big man's arms—"are just shy of pretty, but they pay good for light-colored hair deep in Mexico." He crossed to Miriam Hawes and Josie. "This little girl will bring the most."

"What about her mother?" Powers asked.

Bethea reached out to touch Miriam's shoulder. She

stepped back. "It's a long ways to where we're goin'. I can tell by lookin' at her she's got enough grit to keep the others alive."

"And the old woman?"

"Only slow us down." Bethea nodded to the man who stood over Gladys Jean. "Kill her."

A pistol shot rang out. Josie screamed.

More hands grabbed my arms and spread them out over the wheel. Ropes lashed my wrists to the iron rim. A loop of rough hemp bound my elbows to the spokes and circled my neck, wedging my head against the wagon. With each breath I took, the rope tore at the skin on my neck. Bethea's men skidded Smitty's body so close to me that his lifeless fingers rested on my thigh. They heaved the old woman so that her head pressed my hip.

Riders filed into the camp. I counted fourteen in all. Powers passed whiskey bottles around. Rough hands pushed June and the other women close to a wagon. They huddled there in each other's arms. Hushed whispers filtered out between their sobs.

From the canyon rim a wolf's howl filled the valley.

The giant snapped up his rifle and trained it at the canyon top.

"Settle down, Gatlin," Powers said. "That wolf smells blood." He looked at me tied among the dead bodies. "It knows it'll eat well tonight."

I pulled on the ropes that bound me. They only dug deeper into my skin. "Burn in hell, Powers."

I summoned up what moisture I could find in my mouth and spit. The glob splattered on his shiny boot.

Two steps brought Powers to the wagon where I sat tied to the wheel. With the same boot I'd spit on, he kicked my ribs. Gristle tore from the bone. Bile filled my throat. Powers reared back to kick again.

Bethea stopped his foot with the barrel of his rifle. "No. He's mine to toy with." He nodded toward the covered wagon. "Show me the gold."

Bethea jerked his head for the giant to follow him. He tapped the wagon box with his rifle butt. "This where you hid the gold, Powers?"

"There's twenty bars twice as big around as a man's wrist and a foot long hidden under the floorboards. Ten of those are mine." Powers's fingers tapped the rifle barrel. "That's what we agreed on."

Gatlin pulled the torn canvas aside. Standing flat-footed, the giant reached over the sideboards. He caught hold on the floorboards and heaved up. Nails sung out at the strain.

A high-pitched snarl cut the air. Gatlin jerked his hand back. Flecks of his blood flew from his hand. Trooper yipped.

"What is it?" Bethea said.

"Damn dog got me." Gatlin's voice was slow and heavy. He climbed on the wheel spokes with his knife in his fist and stabbed down. Trooper dove over the side of the wagon and made for the skunkbrush in the shade of the canyon walls. Bethea jerked his Winchester to his shoulder. He snapped off a shot at the fleeing dog. Dust jumped behind Trooper.

Gatlin lumbered around the end of the wagon. He licked the blood from the tooth marks on the back of his hand and stroked his knife blade on the front of his pants.

"Forget the dog. We'll tell the Apaches where it's hiding. They might want to cook up somethin' to eat when they get here."

The outlaw leader tapped the wagon with the barrel of his rifle.

"Show me that gold."

Gatlin lifted his bulk into the wagon. Lumber creaked and snapped. A smile curled the corners of Gatlin's mouth. A reflected sunbeam flashed off his face. He squinted and lifted the gold bar. It seemed small in the giant's hands, but his muscles knotted at its weight.

"Nineteen more just like that," Powers said. "I put 'em there myself."

Gatlin handed the gold to Bethea.

"Have your man count out ten of those for me." Powers pushed back his Stetson. "The Swede and me will load our share on two of the mules and be leavin'. I did what I promised."

"Sit tight." Bethea never looked up from the gold. He turned so the rifle in his free hand pointed at Powers's middle.

I wanted him to pull the trigger and kill Powers like he'd shot down Gladys Jean.

"I'm gonna send Solo to find Victorio," Bethea said. "This is as good a place as any to do our tradin'. I'll have some of my boys hide in the rocks with their rifles in case things don't go as they should. Might need you and the Swede."

"I kept my side of the bargain. Brought you the gold and the women." Powers stepped back. "I want what's mine." Sweat streamed down his face from the hatband of the black Stetson.

"What's troublin' you, Powers?" Bethea touched his lips to the gold bar. "Don't you trust my word?"

Flies feasted on the death around me. Their hum tortured my ears. Ants dashed onto my face to carry off flecks of dried blood. I no longer tried to chase them away with a twitch of muscle or a puff of breath. The sun had robbed my strength. I willed moisture to my mouth, but none answered. Only a glimpse of June by the wagon stirred what strength that remained inside me.

Powers took a long drink from a canteen. He splashed water in his hand and rubbed his wet fingers over his face. Rivulets dripped onto his shirt.

My tongue craved what fell in the dirt around his boots.

Powers crossed to the wagon where I was tied. He tilted back the canteen and studied me over the top. He bent forward and set the canteen six inches from my outstretched feet. He nudged it with the toe of his boot and walked away as the water trickled out.

It was the middle of the afternoon when the Indian Bethea called Solo rode back into the canyon. The brand on his horse's flank showed it had been stolen from the army. The knife Solo had held to my throat hung with a brace of pistols from his belt, and he rested a new Winchester across a Mexican saddle.

Powers had said Bethea was bringing fifty of the new rifles with him. He and thirteen of his men each carried one. That meant there were three dozen in the boxes lashed to the pack horses they'd led into camp. Thirty-six rifles to trade to Victorio and his renegades.

Then, as if the shadows came alive, Apache warriors stood where nothing had been before. Two slipped from the brush near the seep where we had watered the mules. Two more stood near the slabs of fallen rock. An Apache with an old musket crept up beside Powers and snatched his new Winchester before the man could pick it up.

From beneath the wagon where I was tied, another Apache slithered like a lizard over Smitty's body. His eyes studied me, like a vulture would look at a carcass.

Muffled slaps of hooves on dirt drifted over the silence that took control of the camp. June raised her head to look my way. She cringed when she saw the Apache crouched near me.

Three Apaches on gaunt ponies rode into our camp. The horses' hooves had been wrapped in leather so they made scarcely a sound on the rocky ground.

Bethea stood from his place in the shade of the wagon with his treasures. He lifted his Winchester over his head with both hands. "Victorio, you honor me. The rifles I promised are here. But first I have whiskey for your warriors."

Gray showed in the leader's black hair. He slid from his pony's back. On the ground his bowed legs seemed too short for his body, better suited for the back of his horse. "Rifles before whiskey," Victorio said.

"You bring the Mexican coins?"

"Rifles . . ."

"Show me the gold."

"Show rifles."

Bethea lowered the rifle from over his head. He half turned and tucked the gunstock under his arm. "Boys," he lifted his voice.

Along the rim of the canyon, six of Bethea's men stood from where they had hidden in the rocks. Each held his rifle across his chest.

Victorio eyed the marksmen, then jerked his head. From

the cracks and creases on the opposite canyon wall, twice as many Apache warriors showed themselves.

Bethea's laugh boomed. "Gatlin, kill the fattest mule. Build up the cook fire and bring out the whiskey. We got gun tradin' to do."

Chapter Seventeen

The sun moved across the patch of sky between the canyon walls. It would be hours until it dropped far enough to shade the wagon where I was tied. Strength ebbed away with each minute that passed. Like a gambler watching cards dealt on a poker table, I waited for what would come.

Along the iron wheel rim beneath my left hand, my fingers found a rough burr in the metal. Some rock in the miles of trail had scored the wheel. I curled my wrist so I could move the rope over the sharp metal splinter. A single fiber in one strand gave way. In a motion no larger than the thickness of a deck of playing cards, I began to saw at my bindings. I strained back and forth, and the second fiber tore. The sun sucked moisture from my lips, and more than a minute later, the third thread broke.

Victorio and the two warriors who rode in with him sat cross-legged on a piece of sun-splashed dirt. Bethea and Powers knelt across the fire pit from them. Slabs of meat from the mule's haunches hung over the fire. Bethea sipped at a whiskey bottle, but when he held it to the Apaches, Victorio raised his hand and refused to let his warriors take the bottle.

The leader never touched the new rifles. He stared straight ahead while his two chiefs, with bits of half-cooked meat dangling from their mouths, worked the rifles' actions and snapped the triggers.

At Bethea's nod, Gatlin lifted a blanket from the back of one of the wagons. Boxes of cartridges had been stacked in the wagon box. But Bethea refused to bring the ammunition near the guns.

Victorio took two gold coins from a pouch on his belt. He tapped a rifle with the coins. Bethea shook his head and raised five fingers. Victorio's chest swelled with a deep breath, and he brought out a third coin and held it with the first two. Again, Bethea shook his head. He nodded for Solo. Bethea's Comanche brought three more bottles of whiskey from a wagon and set them on the ground in front of the Apaches.

Victorio frowned and held the three coins over the rifle.

Bethea held up four fingers.

Victorio struggled to his feet. He pushed by Bethea's men guarding the women. Josie buried her face in her mother's lap. Victorio stepped by them and tangled his hand in Veronica's hair. He played the blond strands through his fingers. Tears formed in the woman's eyes, and a sob came up from deep inside her.

June bolted to her feet. She slapped Victorio's hand away from her new friend's hair. Hands on her hips, she looked the Apache in the eye. His lips turned up in a crooked smile and his hand shot forward, grabbing the front of her dress. June tried to move away, but the fabric tore. Victorio snatched a new grip on the ruined dress, brought June to his side, and wrapped his forearm around her throat, lifting her from the ground.

I jerked forward on the ropes and screamed, "No!" I sawed the rope back and forth on the rough metal. But the iron splinter snapped away, and the ropes slid over the rim without tearing.

The Apache turned to Bethea. "Five for rifle." Victorio dragged June away from the other women, the tips of her toes trailing over the dirt while her fingers clawed at the Indian's bare arms. Blood filled the scratch marks, but the Apache never flinched. He pointed to the ammunition on the wagon. "This woman and bullets, too."

The same smile I'd seen on Little Jed's face when he dared me to kill him curled the old man's lips. Bethea looked away from Victorio and found my eyes. "Deal's done."

The Apache snatched up a whiskey bottle. The amber liquid spilled from his chin onto June's torn dress as he gulped down a mouthful. She wrestled to free herself, but he held her tight.

One of his war chiefs went to his horse and returned with a heavy leather bag. While Victorio swigged more whiskey, his warrior counted out the coins.

Gatlin heaved two wooden crates onto his massive shoulders and brought them to where the others sat. When the pouch of gold was pushed in front of Bethea, Gatlin slid the rifles to the Apaches.

My muscles fought the ropes, but the hemp held tight.

"He your man?" Victorio pointed to me.

I pulled harder.

June bobbed her face up and down. "Save him from Bethea and I'll go with you. I'll be your woman."

Victorio pushed June to arm's length, his fingers tangled in the whiskey-wet place on her dress. His dark eyes seemed to bore into her. Skin as dark as ancient rust trembled. As quick as a lizard's tongue, he cracked the back of his hand across June's face.

I screamed out again. The rope tore at my throat.

He cocked his hand to strike again. A whimper rose from June's throat. She wrapped both arms around her stomach and twisted her face away.

His hand dropped to his side. The Apache leader's head tilted back, and the noontime sun washed over his face. "I pay for her with much gold." His voice echoed down the canyon.

The sun refused to move another inch across the sky. Blood seeped from my wrists, and my muscles knotted. The sounds of June's gasps filled my ears. My mind searched for what to do next. Nothing answered.

"Gatlin, have them Mexican boys dig a hole." Bethea hefted the bag of gold and pointed to a sandy patch of ground near the end of the wagon. "Make it as deep as a grave."

The giant took a shovel from one of the wagons and lumbered off.

Bethea crossed to where I was tied. He dropped onto one knee. "I was gonna let my Comanche peel the skin off you an inch at time and then build a fire under your belly. Roast you like a fat deer. But that's too good for you." He tapped my leg with the barrel of his rifle. "I've got new plans for you." He rocked back as if he was going to stand and then pounded his fist into my face.

Blood clouded my eyes, and flies swarmed in to feast on the smear. The sound of a shovel turning dirt for my grave mixed with June's sobs.

"You men hitch up that wagon. Burn everything we ain't takin'." And Bethea turned his back to me.

The wagons were ransacked. Crates smashed open. Shovels, picks, and drilling hammers were flung on the ground. Whiskey bottles passed hand to hand.

Bethea's outlaws brought mules to the wagon. Harnesses slapped over the animals' backs. Gatlin lifted Josie Hawes and her mother into the wagon in one motion. He caught Veronica around the waist. She reached out toward June, but the giant tossed her over the torn canvas and into the wagon.

In the confusion around me, Victorio led June to their horses. He lifted her onto one's back and tied her hands together with a length of leather.

She twisted to see me. The welt from Victorio's blow blossomed on her face. "Kepler." Her voice was more precious than the water I craved.

"Do what he says, June. *Stay alive.*" *Just stay alive.*

Too much time without water had taken its toll. My head lolled against the ropes that held me to the wagon wheel. Flies landed on my eyelids and skittered over my lips, the beat of their wings vibrating in my nostrils.

Ants found their way into every wrinkle on my shirt and fold in my flesh. Like ten thousand stabs from red-hot needles, their stings set my skin on fire.

Flames licked the wagons. Black smoke fouled the air.

"Solo," Bethea bellowed and pointed at me.

The Comanche tossed a whiskey bottle aside and motioned for two of Bethea's men. He pulled his scalping knife from his belt.

My breath caught in my chest and refused to move in or out. Solo touched his knife blade to my neck. I braced for it to bite and slash my throat. But the sharp edge caught the rope that tied me to the wheel spokes, and in a quick motion he cut through it. The outlaws with him cut away the ropes that held my hands and arms to the wheel. They pulled me to my feet. Blood rushed through my veins to muscles that had too long been cramped. My knees buckled, but the two held me up.

My arms were jerked behind my back. The rope they had freed me from was wound around my wrists. They dragged my limp legs through the dust and dropped me into the grave that Bethea had ordered the Mexican boys to dig. I turned my head and looked up.

Bethea knelt at the hole's edge and stared into my eyes. The same cruel smile still curled on his mouth. Solo took up a shovel and scooped dirt into the hole and onto me. I fought to sit up. The next shovelful hit full in my face. Dirt filled my eyes and mouth. I spit it out. More came. I tumbled onto my back and twisted to avoid the next. Dirt fell on my chest. More on my legs. Pebbles and rocks pelted down. Through the dust in my eyes, Bethea's unchanging, cold face watched my confusion turn to terror.

June called my name. Her voice was clear over all else. More than the fear of death, the thought that I could do nothing to save June sank its teeth the deepest.

I fought against the ropes and tried to sit. I needed to see June. Her face, not Bethea's, before the ground swallowed me.

Suddenly Solo reached down and caught me by my shoulders. He jerked me out to the edge of the hole.

"Kepler!" June screamed.

Bethea laughed. "You think about her, Kepler. When Victorio is tired of her, he'll trade to one of his warriors for the next swallow of whiskey. With one of them gruntin' on top of her, she'll be cryin' out your name." He nodded.

Solo cocked his shovel over his shoulder. And it swung toward my face.

Pain burst into a white light. Then only darkness.

Chapter Eighteen

Ants.

Ants swarmed over my face.

They filled my mouth. Skittered across my nose.

I tried to shake my head. I couldn't move it. Weight crushed my chest. Pinned my arms and legs so not one fiber of muscle could stir.

Only my eyelids moved. Dying flames flickered on the rubble that had been the wagons. Smoke mingled with the smell of blood and fresh dirt.

I fought to move an arm. A hand. Even a finger. Earth crushed down on me. Slowly my mind started to comprehend the horrors one by one.

Bethea had buried me. Only my head was above the ground.

The scream of an animal in death's grip filled the night. And it came from my own mouth.

Trooper?

June's dog. Its tongue touched the scraped and bloody places on my face. It wiped away the ants. I could feel it, like a doctor's salve, begin to heal me.

Other animals were near. Their footfalls trembled through the dirt that held me. I fought to turn to see them. To see Trooper. I couldn't.

Then he snarled and barked. Another animal cried back in fear.

Trooper curled up around my face. The fur on his hip brushed my cheeks, and I rested my head there. Warmth flowed through me, down to the lowest reaches of the earth that held me captive.

Something like sleep took hold of me.

"Landa Goshen! Corporal Taylor, lookee here."

My eyes fought to open in the bright light.

"God in heaven. It's alive."

Vibrations thudded through the dirt.

"Mister Kepler, that you?"

Then, "You men help me dig him outta here."

"Get water."

"Just use your hands. No shovels. Careful, now."

"Not too fast. Just sip that."

Cool water poured down my throat. A damp rag wiped over my face. A knife blade tugged at the rope around my wrists.

"You lay still, hear me? Got the men makin' up some soup for you to eat. It's just jerky meat in boiled water. It help put some salt back inside you. You's near dried out as an old saddle."

My eyes opened. White teeth in a black face looked down at me. "Taylor?" I croaked.

"Yes, suh. Now don't talk no more. Save what strength you got."

"No. June. Help, we need to find her." I caught the

137

front of his shirt in my hand and pulled to sit up. Lightning snaps of pain fired in every joint and muscle.

Taylor peeled away my fingers and laid my arm beside me. "Rest, suh. I got men out lookin' for sign. We'll get your lady back."

"How?" I coughed. "How did you find me?"

"When the mines wagons didn't show up in Tombstone, they sent us out to look. Would never found you 'cept this big ole wolf kept showing itself on each next ridgeline. Like it wanted us to follow 'im." He touched his wet kerchief to my face and flicked away grains of dirt. "Smelled smoke when we got into the canyon and found the wagons that the Apaches burned. Just by luck, Truman saw you. He thought it just a head layin' in the dirt. Fresh wolf sign all around you. Don't know how you made it, suh."

"Trooper." I tried to raise up onto an elbow, but Taylor pushed me down again. "June's dog saved me. It scared off the wolves last night. Did you find him? He's here somewhere."

"Suh"—Taylor rubbed the back of his hand across his mouth—"we found the dog out yonder. Apaches snapped his neck, split his belly open, and tossed him in that spring to foul the water. Wasn't that little dog last night. He'd been dead for more than a day."

Chapter Nineteen

Mother found me in that place that was not quite sleep. She drifted into the stupor that had held me tight since Taylor's men saved me from Bethea's grave. Her fingers picked grains of sand from my cheeks and forehead, touched the raw places on my skin, and she kissed each bruise on my face. From the very edge of the shadows, her touch became words, and she reminded me that strength never comes from force, but from the determination inside.

As she left me, Mother pressed my hand into June's icy fingers. But June slipped from my grasp. Her screams, as shrill as an infant's cries, drowned out by the shouts of Apache warriors and the drunken laughter of outlaws.

The fever that seared through my mind beckoned Landry to rise from her place in deepest hell. She dared not touch me, but she lingered close and her breath stung every insect bite on my skin. From just beyond the ring of light cast by a campfire, she danced for all of Satan's imps.

From someplace far away a wolf lifted its voice, and its pack joined in.

My screams saved me from the dream.

I awoke with my fingers tangled in Taylor's shirt and his strong hands pinning my shoulders to the ground.

"Kepler," he called from miles away. "Kepler." He was calling me from the nightmare.

Hacking coughs blended with words that made no sense. I struggled to sit up. Taylor pushed me down again.

"Drink this," he ordered.

A tin cup poured liquid over my tongue. Fire burned and hit the bottom of my stomach.

"Now the water, suh. Just sip it."

I made the words into a question. "How long?"

"You been rollin' with dreams all night and most of the day. We been pouring whiskey and water into you the whole time."

"No." A cough racked my chest. "How long has June been gone?"

"As best as we can figure, three days, suh."

My muscles trembled and gave way. I fell back on the blanket. Three days?

Fever burned. Landry twirled at the edge of firelight, wolves howled, and the women in my dreams captured me again.

"More water, suh?"

"Please."

"Just a sip, now. Too much make you powerful sick."

Cool fluid flowed down my throat and tumbled into the pool in my stomach. Water seeped into my aching muscles. Liquid moistened sinew and tendons. It found the places in my joints and let them move again. Finally the water found its way to my mind. It washed the clouds away like grime on a dusty window glass until thoughts became clear.

I raised myself on an elbow. "How long?"

Taylor measured each word. "Miss June been gone five days now."

We sat for a long time in the shade of the canyon walls. Taylor made me drink broth made from boiled jerky and coaxed me to eat bits of hardtack.

"Do we know where they took her?" I struggled to stand. Taylor caught my shoulder and pushed me down.

"I know you want to find her. But you rest. Sent scouts to follow their trail," Taylor answered. "'Pears they headed back around north. Like dey goin' back to dose mountains above Vengeance. Scouts say Apaches and Bethea's men, they ride together. Can't figure out why."

"June?"

"She and dose other women still with 'em."

"You have to go with me and help get her back."

"Ain't but got seven men. Eight counting you. Bethea and the Apaches got more than eighty. Scouts say more joinin' 'em every day." Taylor held out a canteen.

I shook my head.

"You take it, suh. Dis water heal you."

No. I needed June. Only having her with me could take away all the pain.

Taylor pressed the canteen into my hands. "Savin' Miss June's a job for every company of cavalry General Crook can put after 'em. Or a couple good men could follow until they find a chance to sneak in and steal her away. Right now, we ain't near enuf and eight of us is too many." Taylor looked away. "I gots to get back to Vengeance and report in. My orders."

"Then I'll go after her by myself."

"Knew you'd say that." He shook his head. "You ain't got no gun. No horse. No supplies."

"I'll take yours. Steal them if I have to."

"Knew you'd say that, too."

"It's my fault." Bethea had buried me alive. But the thought of losing June tortured me more. "I was trying to get her out of Vengeance when this happened. I'm the reason." I struggled to stand. To go after her on foot. Without a gun or knife if I had to.

Taylor grabbed my arm and lowered me to the ground. "I just been in Arizona a little time," he whispered to me. "Top sergeant, he sends us out in twos to scout for these freight wagons that supposed be at the fort, but hadn't come in. Me and Trooper Moses—"

I remembered the wooly white hair peeking out from under the old soldier's cap before the slug from an Apache carbine burst his head. The taste of the trooper's blood and brains once again settled on my tongue.

Taylor went on. "We ride out as far as Sergeant tell us. It hot that day. No shade at all. There's this tall ridge. I tell Moses I gonna ride up there. Have a look before we turn back. He tell me, 'no.'" Taylor hung his head. "Next day, top sergeant he lead us out that way. We find dose wagons. Apaches got 'em first. Tied the teamsters to wagon wheels and burned 'em up. If I woulda ride up that ridge I might been able to signal wagons, maybe get the troop out there before the Apaches get to 'em."

Taylor lifted his head, found a place near the rim of the canyon, and stared. "Top sergeant, he know what I thinkin'. He tell me this. Lord Jesus and his disciples come on dis blind man beggin' by the side of the road. They ask the Savior, 'Why dis man blind? Did he sin or was it the fault of his parents that he be blind?'" He knotted his hands together, as if to pray, as he watched the sky above us. "Jesus didn't answer at first. He spit on the ground and made mud.

He smear the mud on the man's eyes and tell him to go wash it off. When the man come back, he can see."

"Why tell me this fable? It won't help me get June back."

"'Cause of what top sergeant say next." Taylor looked down at me. "Jesus say, the blind man didn't do nothing wrong. His parents didn't sin. The man was blind so he'd be there beside the road that day and Jesus would find him and do the miracle. Sometimes, God lets the bad happen, 'cause He's got a bigger plan."

I raged at Taylor's words. In all my life I'd heard the disheartened talk of God's plan but as an excuse for unexplainable loss. "Foolish talk for children, that's all it is. If your God let those cutthroats steal June, explain the reason for what they're doing to her right now." Bethea's promise that June would be sold to the next savage for a swig of whiskey drove my rage higher. I struggled to my feet. Every muscle and joint screamed its protest. "I'm going after her. Don't try to stop me."

Taylor didn't move. "I call my horse General. You take him, suh. Gotta Springfield we'll give ya. Men split up some of their ammo for you to take." He rubbed his mouth. "Be dark soon. Best to ride in the cool."

Taylor helped me to my feet.

He slipped his hand inside his shirtfront and came out with a scrap of paper. "Made dis. It's a kinda map. I mark down what the scouts tell me. It might help you find her."

I took the paper.

"One more thing. All that time Miss June spend at the doctor in Vengeance sittin' with Sergeant Pope. Pope, he hear what the Doctor tell her." Taylor's eyes found mine. "Miss June got a baby inside her. Your baby, Kepler."

I left the troopers as dusk touched the canyon rim. I took a borrowed horse, a rifle, and Taylor's promise to pray for me.

Too many thoughts fought their own battle in my mind. What good was a single-shot rifle against fifty Apaches? Could Taylor's prayers guard me from Landry's evil?

Again and again, I heard Bethea's hand crack across June's face while her arms shielded her stomach.

Why had June kept the news of the baby from me?

Did she think I wouldn't welcome our child? Was I so intent on my hunt for Landry and her wolves that I ignored the precious gift right in front of me? I wanted to believe Taylor's prayers would keep June and the child safe until I could find them.

But something deep inside would not let me.

The desert night closed in around me. I rode all night, rested in the heat of the day, and rode again. I followed the scratches on Taylor's map and kept to the faint trails at the rimrock, trading the chance of being seen for minutes. On the third day, as dawn etched the east, I turned Taylor's horse to follow the mesa top. He balked and shied at the pull of the reins. I tried again. The horse refused.

Instead of heeding his caution, I raked my spurs over the animal's sides. He crow-hopped and turned a tight circle. His nostrils flared, and white ringed his eyes.

In the next instant, the stench of death and blood filled my nose. I had smelled it before. At the torn body of Little Jed in the corral behind Thomas's house. And on the mountain in Colorado. Where I'd faced Landry and her master.

I snatched the rifle from its scabbard.

"Whoa, General," I told Taylor's horse. He side-stepped and tossed his head.

I scanned the shadows' edges and searched the rocks and brush. Would it be wolves or warriors in the shape of wolves waiting there to pounce?

General fought the bridle.

"Easy, there," I said, hoping my voice would soothe his instinct to bolt.

The horse backed off four steps. I pulled the reins tight until General's chin touched his chest. His fear stirred under the saddle.

"Now, now."

If he ran, I doubted I had the strength left to hold him.

Streaks of crimson and orange crept over the horizon and spread over the red dust of the trail. Hoofprints from General and another horse filled the dirt. The pattern showed that the other animal had followed the trail to this spot. The horse had balked, made tight turns, and fought its rider to flee. Hoof marks on the trailside painted a picture of a runaway horse. There I saw the first boot prints.

I turned General away from the smell that hung all around us, dropped from his back, and tied the horse to a twisted piñon tree.

The sun inched above the horizon, chasing the shadows to the edges of the brush and rocks. No more than two long steps from where I had seen the wolf tracks, I found the first blood. Scraps of saddle leather were scattered over the ground, and tattered bits of a Navajo blanket hung in the brush. My mind conjured a picture of a wolf leaping to grab the rider from the horse's back. I pulled back the hammer on the Springfield.

More blood pooled in the hoofprints, and the scent in

the air settled like oil on my tongue. I saw where the horse had stumbled and lost its rider. More blood. So much that the thirsty desert sand had drunk its fill and great splotches of red pooled on top.

I found the horse first. Hamstrings torn away from both legs, neck snapped, and belly ripped open for the wolves to feast on its entrails. The smell of musk and blood flowed from my nose into my stomach, and I fought the rush of bile up my throat.

I imagined how the monsters had toyed with the man. The tracks showed they trotted after him, perhaps stopping to lick his horse's blood from their faces each time the man fell. I found an empty pistol where he had turned to fight.

But lead bullets will not kill this kind of wolf.

I eased down the hammer on the Springfield. Nothing I had would protect me from what had killed this poor soul.

Flesh-stripped bones shined in the new sun. To one side, hollow eye sockets and an open mouth on the castaway skull hinted at this man's terror. I tied a kerchief over my nose and mouth to protect me from the stench that hung all around me. With Little Jed, the fight had taken only seconds before Landry tore him to pieces. The tracks here showed six or more had played this game.

Off to the side of the trail, in the brush, the man's left arm hung in a fork in the branches. It had been torn loose just below the elbow. Every other bone had been picked clean of all skin and muscle, but here the skin had not been touched. A ray of sun glimmered off the turquoise nuggets in a heavy, hammered silver Navajo bracelet that circled the wrist.

My stomach rebelled, but I forced myself to retrieve the severed arm. I had touched corpses before, but none had been as cold as this dead man's arm. The silver bracelet had spared this one piece from the wolves' savagery. Perhaps this trinket could protect me.

What other hope did I have?

Taylor's horse snorted. Tree branches snapped as he strained to pull free. From below the rim, another horse snorted back.

I heard voices. Not the words, only the sounds.

I snatched the dead man's pistol from the ground and stuffed it into the front of my belt. His saddlebags and canteen lay near the ruined body of his horse. I slung them over my shoulder as I dashed by and dove for cover in a cluster of rocks. Flies buzzed near my face and settled on the bloody stump of the severed arm.

General thrashed. Tree branches cracked and the horse trotted toward where I hid, trailing his reins in the dust. General tossed his head and his nostrils flared at the invisible barrier of the stench. He stopped and stared at me.

The sound of unshod hooves came closer. General could give away my hiding place. I snatched up a rock as big as my fist and hurled it at the horse. General flinched as the rock smacked his hip. He turned and trotted into the piñons.

I pushed the saddlebags into a cleft in the stones, bellied against the rocks, and lifted just enough of my face so that I could watch the trail.

Heat from the rising sun warmed the blood on the ground. The dead horse's guts swelled with the warmth. Coaxed by the smell, waves of black flies came to feast there.

The first rider, mounted on a black and white paint, came into the clearing and paused. The three who followed him reined their horses to a stop. Through the trees I could see their horses' bellies and legs but not the men on their backs.

I pulled my hat from my head and jammed it under my stomach lest a gust of wind might catch it and give away my hiding place. I thumbed back the hammer on the Springfield with just enough pressure on the trigger to stave off the click that could betray me.

More voices. The horses moved toward me. I studied each glimpse of the horses' legs and tails. These were scraggly pintos. Ribs showed in their sides, and their uncombed tails touched the ground. I spotted a rider's leg against his horse's bony side. Yellow stripes on faded blue from a cast-off pair of army breeches covered his legs.

They stopped their horses. Voices lifted in a jabber of excitement.

They'd found the tracks.

I searched my mind trying to remember where I'd stepped. Would they be able to tell my boot prints from the dead man's?

More chatter. I made out the guttural tones of the Apache language. Their horses clustered around the tracks in the trail. The lead rider swung his mount away from the others and walked a few steps down the trail toward the dead horse, the man's body, and where I hid.

I saw the knife on his hip before I saw his chest and face. It was Solo. He'd held that razor-edged Bowie to my throat while Bethea bargained for the rifles with Victorio. Now he rode with three Apaches.

When Taylor gave me his crude map, he said that Bethea's men and Victorio's Apaches rode together. Solo and these three were on some scouting mission for the larger group. June would be with them.

In his horse's next step, I could see Solo clearly. I shrank tight against the rock and willed every muscle in me to be still.

The renegade Comanche pointed at the bloody splotches on the ground and the carcass of the horse. The others joined him as he slipped from his horse's back. One poked with his foot at the intestines bulging from the horse as a boy might test the edge of a mud puddle with his shoe. He swatted at the flies that rose in protest.

But it was what they did when they found the dead man that chilled the deepest places in my soul.

Solo fanned the air in front of his nose as one might lift the fragrance of a flower closer to be enjoyed. A smile as vile as the one on his face when he'd held his knife to my throat twisted the corners of his lips. The others pointed at the carnage and chattered as if they were counting each piece of torn flesh and the scattered bones.

Solo signaled, and the last of his followers gathered sticks and built a fire on the bloodstained ground just yards from where I hid. With a swipe of his knife, Solo cut a chunk of meat from the dead horse's haunches and set it to roast over the new campfire.

I could only watch as the four of them knelt by the fire, feeding on strips of the half-cooked horse meat and celebrating the death that had happened here. The buzz of ten thousand flies blended with their laughter.

Not daring to lift my head enough to sip from the dead man's canteen, all I could do was watch. Finally, with bellies full, the riders gathered their horses and moved away. Solo was last in the single line. He paused, swung down from his horse's back, and snatched the man's skull from the ground. He held it like a trophy for the others to see and then tied it to his belt with a leather thong, got back on his horse, and rode away.

When the sounds of their horses had dropped from the rimrock to the valley, I pulled the canteen from where I'd hidden it and drank my fill of its warm water. I moved from the sun to where a splash of shade near the trees promised a bit of cool. But the promise was a lie.

I dumped the man's saddlebags out on the dirt. The contents were what I'd expect a wandering cowboy might carry—a half box of cartridges for the pistol I'd found, a straight razor wrapped in a bit of cloth, a clean but faded homespun shirt, a blackened skillet and coffeepot, a bit of salt, and some dried beans.

I peeled off my shirt and let the breeze tease the moisture on my skin. My shirt was still stained with the dirt from Bethea's torture. I hung it on a branch and pulled the dead man's clean shirt from his belongings. Tucked in its sleeve, a rolled piece of paper fell into the dust between my boots.

My newspaperman's eyes recognized the paper type first. It was the same stock that Thomas used in Vengeance to print window posters for the shopkeepers along Main Street. His mark was stamped on the back. I unrolled the paper. In bold letters across the top the page, the word "reward" was spelled out.

Beneath the word was a sketch of my face.

Chapter Twenty

Wanted: Dead or Alive

Except, the word alive had been slashed through with a knife blade.

And there was five-hundred-dollar bounty on my head.

The charge: Murder.

For the killings of passengers of the mine wagons.

Their names were listed: Miriam Hawes, her daughter Josie, Veronica, Gladys Jean, Smitty, and the last . . . the woman known only as June.

Anger boiled up inside me.

I scanned the poster again and saw the claim that I had led the wagons into the hands of hostiles. But it was who had posted the reward that fanned the heat of my anger. I slammed my fist into the ground.

The Pinkerton man had put up the reward money.

Orville Powers was as shrewd as a fox. The version of the story he'd told would put the blame on me and shield him. If my body was found in the grave Bethea had dug, no one could challenge him. If somehow I survived, every bounty hunter in the territory would be on my trail.

But what could I do about his lies? Go back to Vengeance to clear my name? How many bushwhackers were braving the Apaches to put me in their rifle's sights? If I made it to Vengeance, what then? My word against a Pinkerton's?

Taylor and his soldiers would explain how they found me in the canyon where Bethea had left me for dead. Would the town believe the words of the black soldiers? Powers would claim Victorio had double-crossed me.

My reason focused.

June.

Only June.

I had to find her. Nothing else mattered.

I pushed every other thought far away and gathered what I could from the dead man's belongings. I tucked his razor into the top of my boot, loaded his pistol, and slipped it into my belt. Still bare-chested, I crossed to the fire the Apaches had built on the blood-soaked earth. I snatched up the remaining morsels of the horse meat they had cooked and gobbled down the greasy, cold meat.

The dead man's dried blood held the turquoise cuff to the severed arm. Using my fingernails, I tore it free of the graying flesh and slid it onto my own wrist. Only then did I pluck the wanted poster from the dirt. It would go with me until the day I could throw it at the feet of Orville Powers and shoot him down.

Over a poker table in a saloon years before, I had used my winnings to buy whiskey to loosen men's tongues. Each shared his reasons to ride this hostile country. They talked of the promise of gold or a piece of land they could have for their own.

My reason now was the strange mixture of love for June and hate for the Apaches, traitors, and outlaws that would keep me from her.

Every minute put June and her captors farther from me.

Should I try to find Taylor's horse? I shook my head, covered my shoulders with the dead man's shirt, and on foot followed the Indians' trail off the mesa.

From the next ridgeline, far away, the lone sound of a single animal reminded me of what more I must face.

A wolf howled.

Chapter Twenty-One

Something other than anger guided me down that steep, broken trail off the mesa. When the last bit of water dribbled into my mouth from the dead man's canteen, I wondered if there would be no answer to Taylor's prayer.

Heat rose in waves from the gravelly soil. I needed rest and I needed water or else my pledge to find June would end. Only the desert could claim the reward on my life.

A man's eyes play tricks when his body is starved for water. The mind conjures relief where none is to be had. I'd heard stories of bodies found holding canteens filled with sand and mouths stuffed with dirt, convinced in the last throes of life that dust was water.

My mind teased me with a sound.

A horse nickered.

I convinced my brain to tell me it wasn't so. But the horse called again and stamped its foot.

I brought the rifle to my shoulder and cocked it, sure that Solo and the renegades who rode with him were waiting. Who else would be in this hell-barren wilderness?

A horse stepped from stunted paloverdes. It was General, Taylor's horse. The saddle was still cinched to his back, and the canteens the soldiers had given me hung from its horn.

I rubbed a dirty hand across my eyes and blinked. General tossed his head.

I sorted my thoughts one by one. A mirage shimmered in the distance, tempting a thirsty man with water, not with a saddled horse standing twenty yards away. It had to be a trick by the Apaches to make me step into the open where they could shoot me down.

General swished his tail to shoo a fly from his face, and he walked toward me.

The Apaches were behind me. They had to be. I swung around, pointing the muzzle of the Springfield at shadows in the rocks and any twitch of a branch.

When I turned back, the horse was just steps away. Water dripped from the canvas on the canteens, and the smell of sweat, manure, and saddle leather found my nose.

"General?"

His ears perked.

"Are you real?"

I reached out and caught hold of his bridle and rested my face on his.

"Where did . . ." I found the first canteen. It was heavy and full in my hands. I pulled it to my lips. The water was cold and clean and poured relief into every part of me.

But how could the canteens be full?

I'd found no place to fill them since I'd left Taylor and his men days before. This water was cold. Not tepid from days in the canteen slung on the horse's back. I took another gulp, wary but desperate.

General's coat had been brushed and curried, as if he'd been cared for by the finest stable in a grand city. He'd been fed. His saddle was oiled and fresh.

There was no reason to it.

Over General's back I checked any place an Apache might hide, then tucked the Springfield into the scabbard on General's saddle and tossed the dusty saddlebags behind the cantle.

I told myself it was Taylor's prayer that had worked this miracle, but when I bowed my head to thank his God, the tracks of a lone wolf showed clearly in the dust.

———————————

Bold marks on Taylor's map labeled a place where men shared in conversations around saloon tables, in stables, and over corral fences. Agua del Escrito was the only dependable water hole between Vengeance and Tombstone. Other water might be there one year and gone the next. Huddled against the great white cliffs, an underground spring bubbled into a shaded pond. Since the time of the conquistadors, desert wanderers had never found it without water.

A tribe of ancients had carved caves into the white sandstone cliffs that stood guard over the spring. For the Apaches, the place was a stopover when they left their mountains to raid into Mexico. The water hole was marked on every map and in the mind of every frontiersmen that crossed this desert.

I'd heard how those who had stopped at the place had left their mark on the rocks that shaded the pools of fresh water. From prehistorics carrying flint-tipped spears to Spanish priests to gold-hungry prospectors, the symbols and signatures of history had been carved into the canyon's walls.

According to the legends, the conquistadors who massacred the Apache women and their children stopped at Agua del Escrito to water their horses just days before the warriors took their revenge at the place called Vengeance.

Even if an Apache warrior could go days without water,

Victorio and his war party would need water for their captives and horses. Agua del Escrito would be where they would go. When Victorio took his renegades to the oasis, June would be with him. If they weren't there now, there would be signs they had been and, perhaps, a clue to where they had gone.

If I used the water in the two canteens wisely, I'd have enough to make it to the spring. A game trail along the edge of the mesa led into the desert. A smudge of white sandstone cliffs hugged the far horizon. A single pair of wolf tracks led the way.

The cold water in General's canteens renewed my tired muscles and poured freshness into my mind. It would be foolish to make a direct path to the water hole. Bounty hunters eager for the reward on my life knew that a lone man in this portion of desert would seek the water. A trap might be waiting for me.

The more I studied the wolf's prints on the narrow game trail, the more I became convinced that it had chosen this secret thread and wanted me to follow. No doubt other trails across the desert led to Agua del Escrito. This wolf had chosen one traveled by animals but not by men.

I could lie to myself no longer. The tracks were Landry's. She wrapped her warmth around my face in the canyon where Bethea had left me to die. She had guarded me until the troopers came. Somehow she had brought General to me and produced icy, cold water in the midst of the desert heat. Now she was leading me to whatever was next.

Was I some part of this creature's plan? Or was I her prey?

My mother had taught me of measured gambles. A risk

the reins. My horse pawed the ground, and anxious sounds of recognition churned from him. I knew he wanted to come to me, but something held him back.

"You've trained him well." Landry watched her wolves sprawl on the bloody ground where Powers had died. "Solo is the only one he would let touch him. Go take care of your horse. Get some rest. We'll leave here in a few hours."

Solo had General by the bridle. Taylor's horse's eyes grew wide and a shriek of fear boiled from deep inside him. Solo stared at me. His lips curled into a smile. He pulled the long Bowie knife from his belt. The razor-sharp blade slashed the horse's stomach. Entrails spilled onto the ground, and Landry's wolves began to feast before General's knees folded.

"Oh, and Kepler," Landry said, "a man only needs one horse."

I turned my back on the orgy of blood and torture. Seer nuzzled my shoulder, as if the horse found comfort to be with me again. Everything in me begged to jump onto Seer's back, put my spurs to his sides, and fell these abominations.

If there was any chance to save June and the child she carried, I would need to go with Landry, watch and learn and wait for my chance. I led Seer to a stand of twisted trees at the far end of the water hole.

I tried to calm him, but his nerves stood on end like mine. There would be little real rest and no sleep for a long time.

Chapter Twenty-Five

S olo came for us.

Night still draped the canyon. He pointed at Seer's saddle and motioned for me to mount up and follow him. He jumped onto the back of a scraggly pinto and rode into the night.

Here and there bits of moonlight won the battle with the darkness and pools of silver bathed the desert. Ahead of us, Landry's eight wolves silently darted between the stunted brush and twisted cactus. They moved like phantoms freed from the captivity of their graves.

I strained to see if Landry was somewhere with the wolves or if she was somewhere ahead, leading the way. But the rules of this world do not govern the fiends who make their home in hell.

Just before first light, Solo pulled up on his horse and raised his arm. He swung down from the pinto's back and lifted a water bag from his saddle. He scuffed out a place in the dirt beside the trail with the toe of his moccasin and poured water into the depression. His horse began to drink from the muddy hole. Solo nodded to me.

I climbed off of Seer's back and let him drink beside the pinto. Solo held out the water bag for me. The bag was made from the speckled skin of a dog, and my stomach turned as I lifted it to my mouth. But the water was cold. I gulped in a mouthful.

Solo pulled the dogskin away from me and sloshed more water onto the ground for the horses.

I caught the last dribble on my chin and smeared it over my dry lips. Seer raised his head from the puddle. I stepped in and caught hold of his saddle's cinch strap and pulled it loose to give the horse a moment more of rest. Over Seer's back I saw the first Apache.

The man was bare-chested and had a scrap of deerskin wrapped around his waist. His long hair was tied back with a strip of leather and bits of leaves and twigs snarled at the ends. I wrapped my hand around the stock of the Henry rifle and slipped a finger over the trigger.

Solo held out the dogskin. The Apache shook his head. The Indian dropped to the ground, stretched out, and rolled up onto one hip. From the bushes nearby, another Apache slithered up near the first. Except for a strip of leather knotted around his forehead, the man was naked. Ribs showed through the skin on their sides, and long, ropey muscles laced their arms and legs.

Seer jerked on his reins and shied away. When I looked down, a third naked Apache was on his hands and knees, beneath Solo's pinto, lapping water from the mudhole.

Over Solo's shoulder two more of the Apaches stood from the brush and walked toward us. Another crawled in from one side, sat up, crossed his legs, and picked with his teeth at a cactus thorn stuck in the skin on his knee.

None of them spoke. They seemed content to rest in the last cool before the day. I counted eight in all.

The same number of wolves had torn Powers apart and ate Taylor's horse alive.

I clamped my eyes shut and shuddered. Even Seer trembled at my thoughts.

It couldn't have been more than thirty minutes before Solo signaled for us to move on. The Apache I had seen first climbed up from where he rested on the ground. He reached out with both arms, his muscles and tendons stretching. He rolled his head from one side to the other. Barefoot, he loped off across the rocky ground. One by one the others stood, stretched their lean, powerful bodies, and trotted after him. Solo mounted his horse and nodded for me to follow.

The sun rose over the horizon and climbed into the skies. Heat bore down from above and welled up from the ground. The sweat that seeped from my skin dried before it could cool me.

The wolfmen-Apaches ran on. Seer struggled to keep the pace, but like me, he seemed to know our only chance to find June was to follow.

Near noon the lead warrior stopped in the shade of a cluster of boulders. His warriors found places among the brush to lie and rest. Their leader climbed to a sheltered place near the top of the rocks. While others slept, he kept watch.

As he had before, Solo poured a bit of water onto the ground for the horses. He gave me a single mouthful from the dogskin. I pulled the saddle from Seer's back, found a place in the shadow of the rocks, and dropped down, too tired to brush the swarming flies from my face.

Beneath the turquoise cuff on my wrist, a single drop of my own sweat clung to my skin. My tongue swept up the bit of wetness and savored the salty taste. I took off the bracelet and summoned the bit of energy I had left.

I pressed the soft silver onto a rounded stone, pushed

down, and let my weight slowly begin to straighten the curve of the bracelet. Little by little, the half circle of silver became a flat piece of metal not quite two fingers wide and as long as from the tip of my thumb to the heel of my hand.

With the last speck of spit from my mouth I wet the stone, and when I was sure Solo had drifted off to sleep, I began to grind away at the edges of the silver. Bit by bit and stroke by stroke, the silver took the shape I wanted. Shiny flecks dropped away until the tip of the metal was as pointed as a saddle maker's awl.

If the chance came, I would stab the silver into her throat with my own hands.

Night crept upon us. Where there had been only heat, the smallest touch of cool moved across my skin. The branches in the brush moved and straightened with the rhythm of a slow waltz. The warrior on the rocks was first to stir. He stood and stretched his cramped muscles.

The seven others rose from the beds they had made on the hard ground. Around each, the waltz of winds became a war dance. It spun, twisted, and twirled, and from each funnel, a wolf pounced. Their leader leaped from the boulder and led them away.

Once, such a sight would have held me in wonder. Now it reminded me of my foolishness. Other men would flee this manifestation of such evil. If I had done so on the mountainside in Colorado, all would be so different. Now I was pledged to follow.

Solo pulled me to my feet. He pushed me toward Seer. We climbed onto our horses and rode after the others. Miles and hours blended. We followed the wolves through the night, and in the morning naked warriors led us to a dry camp in the soft dirt at the bottom of a dry wash. Solo gave what was left of the water to the horses and let me wring the last drops from the dog leather into my parched mouth.

Once I would have memorized every detail for the story I would share with readers. But the praise of editors and dreams of riches were far away from me now. I longed for June and hated Landry. While the others slept, I honed the edge of the silver dagger on a smooth stone.

I blocked the glare from the last rays of the setting sun with my hand and squinted at the growing black shape outlined against the red glow. The Apaches saw it, too. A breeze became a wind. Dust filled the air around us, and eight spinning funnels performed their evil magic. As one, the new night's wolves lifted their voices in a mournful yowl.

With each step the shape from the west grew larger. The wind teased her hair, and her frayed skirt danced on the breeze. Landry had returned to her pack. The leader bounded out to greet her. He reared up. His front paws touched her shoulders and he nuzzled her face. Others joined in, each pushing the next away for its chance to be close to her. Their yips of excitement filled the air. Landry paused to touch one's head, then rub the next one's ear, and give a playful tug on the tail of a straggler.

Surrounded by her underlings, Landry tilted her head back, and from her mouth a howl lifted to the new moon. Each note rose higher than the one before. The wolves' ears perked. Heads tilted and noses sniffed the air. Then the pack raced away toward the setting sun.

"I brought this for you." She held out a canteen as she walked toward me. "I knew you'd be thirsty. I wish it could be as cold as the last I brought you."

When I took it from her and lifted it to my lips, my fingers touched the dark, sticky stains on the canvas cover.

"It's blood," she said. "Victorio's men ambushed a settler's family just over that hill. I sent my wolves to clean up what the Apaches left."

The face of every settler I had seen in Vengeance filled my mind. I pushed away the thought that Fum and his family would be her wolves' meal. I took just enough water to wet my mouth. "You saw him? Victorio?"

"Yes, and June is still with him. He must care for her very much. She's not been harmed."

"Will you take me to her?"

"In time." Landry tilted her head toward some far-off sounds. "My wolves will hunt all night. I'll send Solo to watch over them." She turned to face me and hooked a finger in the front of my shirt. "We'll rest here. Just you and me."

"I'll build a fire." I brushed the dry grass away with my boot and gathered a handful of sticks together. "Night could get cold."

"No." Landry smoothed her gown. The hem was tattered, and pieces of sticks and leaves clung to the folds in the fabric. She found a place on the ground to sit and folded her bare feet under her dress. "I prefer the night. We can watch the stars."

"Where were you?" I took a seat on the ground where I could see her face in the fading light. I crossed my legs and rested my hand near the top of my boot, just inches from the silver dagger I had made. "When I was with Solo and your wolves? What were you doing?"

"Searching." The flash of her teeth told me she enjoyed this game.

"For?" Sometimes the next question would nudge loose the tiniest bit of information.

"Bethea."

"And?"

"Kepler, this is so tedious." She sat upright and stretched her back. "Bethea is a powerful man. I use powerful men."

"Like you used Nicolae?"

Landry's teeth flashed as she laughed. "And like I will use you. That is why you're still alive." She leaned forward and the smallest trace of purple gleamed in her eyes. "Right now Victorio is on his way to meet with Bethea in the mountains above Vengeance. Other Apaches from the north and the east are on their way to join them. Dozens of them. I saw the tracks in the desert. Bethea has more guns to sell. And more than the guns, Bethea has made a promise to the Apaches."

I edged my fingertips closer to the dagger in my boot.

"You know why the Apaches call it Vengeance?" Landry continued. "I'm sure that foolish old man who owned the hotel told you about the legend."

"Saunders?" I remembered the story he told me about the conquistadors' massacre of the Apache women and children. And how a she-wolf led the warriors when they took their revenge. And the promise that the wolf would return to lead the Apaches to their next victory. "Are you the wolf that the Apaches wait for?"

"Bethea thinks I am. That's enough."

"What do you need me for?"

"Bethea does not forgive easily. He blames the town of Vengeance for his son's death." Landry shrugged. "They've joined together, Kepler. Apaches will pay for Bethea's guns. Bethea will pay me to lead the Apaches to attack Vengeance. With money comes power. Power brings fame. I need someone to tell the story. Someone like you."

But Bethea blamed me for killing his son. That's why he'd buried me alive in the canyon. What would he do when he found out I was still alive? Was I another bargaining chip in Landry's game? "What do I get?"

"You get to live. And I'll save your precious June. With the money we'll go to Mexico. Build my own kingdom." She tilted her head like a wolf cub. "Think of it Kepler, you will tell the whole world of my powers."

Or you'll sell me to Bethea to be gutted alive while June watches.

Landry talked through the night of her plans for the palace she'd build in Mexico and of the others like her who would come from the far reaches of the world. She laughed at the bloody games they would play and spoke of abominations that no man would dare imagine.

She answered the howls of her wolves as they returned from their hunt with a call so like the animals' that it disturbed my soul. She greeted each animal as it galloped to her and cradled each monster as it took the form of a man again. Each shared her unholy fervor.

"One more thing." Her warriors struggled to be closest to their mistress. "Before we go up the mountain tonight you must hunt once more," she said to them. "I saw four cavalrymen on patrol this morning. They must not find Bethea's camp."

Could I get a message to them? "Let your wolves rest. Send me instead. Maybe they've returned to Vengeance. If not"—I held up the Henry rifle—"fifteen shots. That's enough for four soldiers."

"They're Buffalo Soldiers, Kepler. Your friends."

"You need to know you can trust me." *Would Landry believe me?*

"Why should I trust you?" It was Landry's turn to ask the questions.

"June." It was the truth. But once June was safe, Landry had to be stopped.

She nuzzled the head of the largest wolf, and without looking at me, she said, "Very well. Solo knows where they will be. I'll send him with you."

Chapter Twenty-Six

Again Solo led me into the night. We left the flat desert floor and the horses labored into the high broken ground. Solo chose the twisted snakelike gulley bottoms, careful to keep off the skyline. Moonlight guided us.

Up one canyon, across the rim, down into the next. With every jolt of the saddle, I plotted a thousand ways to kill Solo, get word to the soldiers, and rescue June. In my heart, I knew none would work. If only Taylor's prayers could be answered.

Seer smelled it first. He tossed up his head.

Solo pulled up on his pinto and dropped from the horse's back to the ground. Smoke from a far-off wood fire tinged the air. Solo tied his horse to the brush and motioned for me to do the same. We bellied up the steep side of the gully.

No more than a quarter mile away, three troopers huddled around a tiny campfire. It was the kind I'd seen Taylor and his Buffalo Soldiers kindle in the desert. A match put to a few branches and dry leaves with just enough flame to boil a coffeepot or warm a skillet of beans. The fourth trooper slouched against a rock with his carbine over his shoulder watching the night and their hobbled horses.

One of the troopers at the cook fire stood and walked out to the sentry. His low voice carried on the calm night air. It was the voice of the man who had promised to pray for me.

A plan began to form in my mind. Whether it was Taylor's God or the turn of the dice, some force of the universe had sent the one man that might believe all the evil I had seen. "Solo," I whispered.

His hand shot up and clamped over my mouth. I pushed it away and motioned for him to follow me back to the horses.

"It will be dawn soon. If we kill them now, the army will send out patrols when they don't report in," I reasoned. "Let's wait to see when they break camp. If they ride back to Vengeance, it will mean they haven't found anything."

His dark eyes took in what I said.

"It's best to wait." I tried again. "Landry would want us to."

Solo nodded. He wriggled up the gulley side and watched Taylor and his men.

I had never shot a man in the back before.

The lack of honor, in those who had, troubled me. Little Jed showed that when he cut loose a shotgun through the bedroom window of Thomas's home. That night he had wanted to kill me, with little concern for whether he hurt June or anyone else in his way. Murder was his motive. Nothing else mattered. The killing shot could come from the front or back.

Solo was a mystery. In the days we'd been together, I had not seen the man take one bite of food, drink one drop of water, or close his eyes to sleep. I remembered him scooping the dead man's bloody skull from the ground and holding it over his head like some trophy.

I suppose I could have called for Solo to turn and face me. Instead, I rested the Henry across Seer's saddle, put the sights between the points of Solo's shoulder blades, and pulled the trigger.

Blue flames flared from the muzzle. The sound shattered the night. The bullet smashed into Solo's back.

A wounded animal's screech, louder than the loudest cannon's roar, ripped open the night. He sprang from the ground and turned to me.

I worked the lever on the Henry and aimed at the center of his chest. The second shot hit as he sprang toward me. Seer reared. I fell back and swung the rifle sideways to protect my face.

Solo pounced on me. I blocked his first swipe at my face and eyes with the gunstock. His fingers wrapped around the rifle and pushed it down across my neck.

I gagged. Fought for air. His full weight crushing my throat. One of his hands came free and grabbed for the long Bowie knife at his belt.

Seer reared and brought his hooves down on Solo's wounded back.

Once. Twice. Three times. Hooves crashed down. The knife flew to one side. Both his hands gripped the rifle. He pressed down.

My fingers found the dagger in my boot. My air-starved brain knew only one thing and I stabbed. Into his ribs. Then his back. And finally I tore at his face.

The force at my neck lessened. I heaved him off of me.

The man that had been Solo twisted in the dust. I poised the knife for my next thrust.

The flicker of firelight washed over the scene. I turned. Taylor and troopers trained their Springfields at Solo. One of the soldiers held a flaming torch. I wrenched it from his hand and stabbed the burning end into the wounded monster.

An inferno erupted. I covered my face and staggered back. The death scream of the animal faded to the moans of a dying man.

Though he'd always walked as a man and never became a wolf, when Nicolae and Landry had risen from the pit of hell, a demonic imp called Solo had crawled up after them.

"Don't shoot." It was Taylor's voice.

When I turned, three cavalry carbines pointed at me.

———————

Taylor shook his head. "Can't be." He pushed a tin cup of barely warm coffee into my hands.

"You saw her. That night behind Thomas's house. You know what she did to Bethea's son."

"I saw a wolf. Can't be sure it was anythin' else."

"You saw Landry as a wolf." I slopped the coffee on the ground and pleaded. "And it was her and her wolfmen at the stagecoach. Stalking us in the desert."

Taylor gritted his teeth and looked away.

"Look at me," I demanded. "Remember the story? The one about how Vengeance got its name? How that some-day a she-wolf will lead the Apaches in a war to win back all they lost?" Taylor shook his head. "Yes, suh."

I reached out, grabbed his shoulder, and turned his face to mine. "Landry told me Bethea has convinced Victorio and the other renegades that she is that prophecy come to life. Bethea's bringing as many Apaches as will listen together. He has more guns. He's planning to use her wolves to lead an attack on Vengeance. He wants revenge for his son. Even if you don't believe it, the Apaches do."

Taylor lowered his head. "We found sign."

"What?"

"Our patrol," he whispered. "We found tracks of six, maybe eight wagons. Heavy wagons. Like they could be loaded with rifles."

"Where?"

"Headed up the back side of the big mesa 'tween here and Vengeance."

"It's Bethea."

"And we spotted Victorio's bunch. Headed that way, too."

"Was June with them?"

"Yes, suh."

"Taylor, if I'm going to have a chance at all to save her, this may be it."

Taylor got down on his knees and drew on the sand with the point of his knife. "We be 'bout here." He made a mark. "We see the tracks of a dozen Apache war ponies here." He pointed. "Here another bunch." His knife scratched the dirt. "Victorio and his warriors, 'bout here." A third mark in the sand. "Bethea's wagons here." He pointed. "And all the tracks headin's here." He reached across and made a half circle in the dust. "Vengeance Mesa."

Taylor sat back. "Sadler?"

One of his soldiers stepped up. "'Member when Sergeant Pope lead us up on dat big mesa 'bout six, seven months ago?"

The man shook his head. "Easy ride up the trail about

here." He touched the butt of his rifle to Taylor's map. "Not hard on the horses, at all."

Taylor eyed me. "Bethea, he take his wagons up that way. Apaches follow him, I betcha." Taylor's knife made another slash in the sand. "Big basin about here. Be room for the wagons and all the horses down in it. The ground in the basin slants down to this steep cliff on the far side. Drops off maybe two hundred feet. Get some men up on the rim with their Springfields, we'd have 'em trapped. Could be a real turkey shoot." Taylor stabbed the knife into the sand. "But if what you say is true, army bullets won't kill Landry and her wolfmen."

I laid the silver dagger on the map. "This will."

"One knife?"

"Can you melt it down and make bullets for the Henry?"

Taylor picked up the dagger and held it out for Sadler to see. "We can. But not many bullets."

"Mold up as many as you can."

"You said Landry had eight apache wolves running with her." He passed the silver blade to Sadler. "We'll try for nine, suh."

"How many might not be as important as how well you can shoot. It may come down to how well you aim that rifle."

The tip of Taylor's tongue touched his lips and he nodded.

———————

Taylor's men built up the fire. Sadler dropped the dagger in a blackened skillet and went to work.

When he was done, the soldier shook his head. "Only eight, suh. Can't make no more."

"Then eight bullets will have to do." I stood up and handed the Henry to Taylor. "I'm going back to Landry. I'll tell her you and your soldiers killed Solo. You pray to that God of yours that she will believe me."

"Miss June? What about her?"

"I'll get to her."

"Suh, once the shootin' starts, it's gonna be real crazy. We won't be able to pick and choose every target."

"I thought of that." But I hadn't. I only knew I had to find a way to save June. "Taylor, pray for me."

"There." Landry pointed to a fresh-chiseled gouge on the pink granite at the side of the trail. "Bethea said he'd leave his mark. We leave the horses here." She climbed from Solo's pinto and tied it to a stunted piñon.

Sweat poured from my face and soaked my shirt. Except for the dust in her hair and the frayed hem of her gown, Landry was as fresh as if she had just sipped from the cold water at Agua del Escrito. No fatigue showed on her eight naked warriors.

I looped the end of Seer's reins to the same tree and glanced back down the steep trail. Our tracks were plain in the dust. Taylor and his men would have no trouble following.

"We need to hurry, Kepler. The sun sets soon. I have a promise to keep." She left the trail and scrambled barefoot over the rocks toward the crest of the mesa. Each of her Apaches hurried after.

I sucked in a breath and fell in at the end of the line. I kicked loose a stone the size of my head. It tumbled to the trail, bounced once, and hurdled down the mountainside.

Muscles in my legs burned. Landry looked back. I stumbled and grabbed a clump of dry grass to keep my balance.

"Tell yourself what grand stories you'll write from what you see today." She bounded from one rock to the next. The wolfmen scrambled after her as if they smelled the blood they were sure to spill.

I pulled the grass from the ground by the roots and let it drop. Twice more I uprooted grass clumps to mark our trail for Taylor.

Landry reached the crest first. She called back to me, "Bethea left us a present." She held up a bottle and sun shined through the whiskey. "Come see. It's just like he promised."

Below us, not a quarter mile away, Bethea's camp sat on the edge of the mesa. He'd found the perfect place to stage his spectacle and guided Landry and her wolves to their place on the rocky stage. At the edge of the cliff, bonfires waited for torches to light the coming night. Two dozen war ponies milled about the wagons and men. Twice as many Apache warriors chanted and danced.

Six wagons clustered near the center, and Bethea's men—maybe fifteen of them—moved out from the wagons shoving bottles of whiskey into the hands of anxious warriors. Crates of rifles were smashed open. The giant, Gatlin, held a new rifle over his head with both hands and marched through the pawing Apaches. Warriors fired into the air with their new guns.

Bethea stood in the back of the closest wagon. He raised a bottle in his fist. Whiskey spilled from his mouth and stained his shirt. From the horde of Apaches, the old chief, Victorio, climbed onto the wagon bed. Gatlin pushed his way through the crowd and tore away the canvas from the top of a covered wagon. The women captured in the canyon struggled to their feet. The cheers from the savages echoed from the mountains.

My heart failed its next beat.

June was last to stand. Her yellow dress was gone and she had been wrapped in a worn scrap of leather. I pushed away the sordid images that battled in my mind. Even with her hands bound together, she covered the precious life she carried inside her.

Bethea leaped to the wagon with the women. He wrapped his beefy arm around June and lifted her from her feet. The rocks around me hummed with the rising noise from the crowd.

Was she to be offered as some prize to these brutes?

I scanned the trail we had climbed for some sign of Taylor and his men. Nothing. I looked along the basin's rim hoping to see one of the Buffalo Soldiers slipping into position with his rifle.

The bottom of the sun touched the crooked hills at the west horizon. Torches were cast in the waiting fire pits. Flames jumped into the sky. Bethea turned to where Landry and her wolfmen waited.

With his signal, Landry stood from her hiding place in the rocks and sprang like a cat to the top of a boulder. One by one, each of her eight followers took his place at the base of the stone.

Now. Taylor, shoot her down.

The wind touched the back of my neck. Dust swirled up from the cracks in the rocks. Currents of air funneled up from the valley floor. Smoke and ash from the fires joined the spiral.

The lower part of the sun slipped below the horizon. Spikes of gold, orange, and blood red stabbed the sky.

Fire the shot, Taylor, before she turns.

Landry's gown tore away from her body and floated into the sky. Arms raised, hair flying, eyes shining as if touched by purple flames, she stood naked before Bethea, the Apaches, and every creature of hell. Lightning stabbed down from the sky. Horses screamed. Thunder rolled up from the valley of the shadow of death.

Torrents of dirt spun tighter around her, and where the woman had stood, a ghostly gray wolf took her place.

Now, Taylor. By all you hold holy, shoot her down.

Landry's eight Apaches lifted their arms to their mistress. Eight whirlwinds dropped from the sky, and as night stole away the sun, eight wolves lifted their voices in a single howl.

Victorio dropped to his knees. Around him, his warriors fell on their faces as the prophecy of the old time unfolded before their eyes. Above their cries, Bethea's laughter roared with the wolves' howls.

The she-wolf bounded from her rocky throne, charging down to greet the fanatics. Eight wolves followed her.

Gatlin pulled Josie Hawes from her mother's arms. He lifted the girl from the wagon bed and held her above his head as Landry's wolves dashed closer. They jumped into the air, snapping at the girl.

June pulled free of Bethea and slammed her full weight into the giant's belly. Gatlin staggered. Josie fell onto the wagon's floor. He caught June by the hair and raised his fist.

Jumping from rock to rock, I hurdled toward the wagons.

Shoot, Taylor. Please shoot.

The first bullet from a trooper's Springfield smashed Gatlin's forehead. A stream of gore shot through the sky. With the next gunshot, Victorio clutched his chest.

I pushed by an Apache. His eyes widened and he pulled a knife from his belt. The third carbine barked, and the warrior dropped in front of me. I shouldered the next, dodging a whiskey bottle swung by one of Bethea's outlaws. A Springfield bellowed, and blood blossomed from a hole in the bandit's throat.

One of Landry's wolves leaped for the wagon with June and the women. A silver bullet from Taylor and the Henry smashed into its side.

Bullets from the Buffalo Soldiers' carbines raked the crowd. A confused outlaw snapped pistol shots into the twilight. A whiskey-addled Apache fumbled with his new rifle. The weapon discharged into the foot of a warrior nearby. In his frenzy to taste blood, one of Landry's wolves leaped onto the wounded man.

A horse pulled free of its tether, and a black wolf sank its teeth into the animal's neck. A bullet from the Henry broke the wolf's back.

Everywhere around me chaos ruled. Outlaws shot their own. Scalping knives slit warriors' throats. Another wolf folded from a silver slug shot from Taylor's Henry. Had Taylor's prayers been answered?

"June!" I screamed and drove my fist into a warrior's stomach. A bullet ripped my shirt and I jumped over a dying Apache. I caught hold of the side of the wagon. Bethea's boot caught me full in the face. I dropped, battling to keep from passing out.

From the ground, I looked up. Dizzy waves shot

through my head. My eyes refused to focus. Bethea's laugh battered my ears.

Bethea shoved June into the other women. They fell hard onto the wagon's floor. His huge hand found the lever for the wagon's brakes. He freed it.

"Tell your woman good-bye."

Bethea jumped down and shouldered into the back of the wagon. Its wheels began to move. He pushed harder. Spokes turned. He heaved his bulk against the wagon box. With the jolt the wagon rolled down the incline to the cliff. Flames from the bonfire caught the trailing canvas.

June and the others clawed at the sides of the moving wagon. They fought to stand. Miriam Hawes was on her feet first. She pulled Josie up and wrapped herself around her daughter and both tumbled over the side boards of the rolling wagon.

Out of the confusion, Taylor was beside me. He jerked me to my feet, turned, and snapped a shot at a charging wolf. Its dying shriek split the chaos.

"Stop it, Kepler," he shouted. "Save Miss June." He clubbed down a knife-wielding thug, worked the lever on the Henry, and fired at the next wolf.

The runaway wagon picked up speed. Its front wheel glanced off the stone fire ring, heaved to the side, and hurtled toward the cliff edge.

Bethea lurched up from behind. Before I could make words come, he knocked Taylor to the ground with his Colt and jabbed the muzzle of his cocked pistol into my stomach. His whiskey breath washed over my face, and he smiled. "For my son." A silver bullet from the Henry exploded his head.

"Miss June." Taylor pointed at the wagon with the barrel of the rifle.

I sprinted to her. Hands still bound together, June helped Veronica over the wagon side. The burning canvas whipped over the two women. Veronica toppled from the rolling wagon, flames twisting in her blond hair.

"June."

I ran with all I had in me.

The wagon's front wheels dropped off the cliff's edge. June fell back and disappeared into the wagon box. Her bound hands gripped the sides, and as she struggled to pull herself up, the wagon tilted farther toward the drop.

The white she-wolf was on me from behind. Her teeth slashed through my shirt and spikes of pain raked my shoulder. She slammed me to the ground. Landry's paws pinned my shoulders there. Blood and spittle drooled from her teeth. I flailed to free myself, but the animal's strength was too much.

I had to see June before I died.

I twisted for a look at the wagon. June pulled herself to her feet. The wagon teetered. It hung for an instant. The earth crumbled. Then gravity's pull won the battle.

Her hands reached out for me and June screamed my name.

I looked into the wolf eyes, ready for Landry's fangs to tear into my face and to let me go to be with June. Instead the wolf's tongue touched my cheek and Landry set me free.

The she-wolf bounded away from the carnage.

Taylor dropped onto one knee and clamped the Henry to his cheek. He sighted down the rifle's barrel and squeezed the trigger. The hammer fell on an empty chamber.

Three black wolves followed their mistress away from the mountain above Vengeance.

Chapter Twenty-Seven

Taylor pulled me from the edge of the cliff. "Don't look, suh."

I pushed him away, fell onto my knees, and clawed the dirt. Splintered boards and scorched canvas littered the rocks. At the edge of the shadows, the spokes from a shattered wheel turned on a broken axle.

The darkness hid June from me.

Taylor touched my shoulder. "It's no use. You'll never find her in the dark. I'll send the troopers in the morning."

"No." And I climbed into the blackness.

I found June on the rocks at the foot of the cliff. Her hands still covered the unborn child inside of her.

I sat with her through the night and thought of what might have been. At dawn, Taylor's men came to help. But I carried her broken body to the mesa top in my arms.

———

Led by the vultures in the sky, a cavalry detachment arrived at midmorning. Jedidiah Bethea's body was among the dead with ten of his outlaws and seventeen Apaches. Only the grace of something greater than any of us had spared the captive women.

When asked about the five dead wolves, Private Freeman Taylor could only shake his head.

Afterword

I trailed Landry and her warriors south and crossed into Mexico. Their tracks turned to rumors, and then only whispers of sightings. At first, I was days behind. Soon a week late. Then a month.

A tired-eyed priest in the village church lowered his face and kissed the rosary tangled in his fingers when he shared the stories he had heard. Indian farmers looked away, and fear showed on the faces of *Federale* soldiers at the mention of an Apache war party led by a she-wolf.

As winter gripped the deserts, I pointed Seer's face north and we road to California. I rented a room in a town in the hills above San Diego to let my body strengthen and allow Seer his rest.

Each day, I scoured newspapers from around the region for stories with any mention of crimes that could be credited to Landry but found not a word. Finally, Freeman Taylor answered my telegram. He explained the army had ceased its search for Landry, and any account of a woman who became a wolf had been stricken from official records.

Thomas, he shared, had reunited with his wife and son. He had sold the newspaper in Vengeance and taken a job in Omaha. When his body healed, Pope had left the army and the one-legged man took up caring for stock for the Wickenburg Stage line. In one bit of news that brought a smile, for his bravery on the mountain above Vengeance, Taylor had been given a promotion. He signed the telegram, "Sergeant Freeman Taylor."

More than anything else, June's loss was my first thought each morning and dared me to sleep each night.

Weeks passed. The mild weather healed my body but not my heart. Seer's coat grew sleek, and a new layer of muscle covered his ribs.

I purchased railroad tickets and booked a place for Seer in a livestock car. It was time to return to where this had all begun.

I found a place in the livery for Seer, flipped the stable boy an extra silver dollar for a double ration of grain for my horse, and, as was my practice when arriving in a new place, left to explore the town.

A feeling of newness hung over this Brokeheart. The last of the winter snow, still in the shade of the buildings along Main Street, shined brilliant, not at all fouled by the ash, dirt, and sins of winter. New paint covered old buildings. Spring flowers crowded together for warmth near the headstones on Graveyard Hill. Near the church, a bell chimed at the school I had help fund for the miners' children.

Where the boardwalk ended, I turned west toward Front Street, where things refused the change. New gave way to a block of shacks and empty corrals. I dodged a wagon and team, and then crossed the rutted street to the Months Saloon.

In spite of the chill in the air, hemp twine tied open the front doors. Workers in railroad stripes shared a table. Miners and teamsters lined the bar.

"Don't get many white shirts in here." Folds of flesh on the arms of the woman behind the bar swung in the same cadence as the newspaper she used for a fan.

"Is the beer cold?" I asked.

"Sugar, even on a day like this, it's warm." Powdered jowls and extra chins framed what had once been a compact face. Gaudy red daubed her cheeks and lips. Limp, graying hair fell across her back to the apron tied at her thick waist.

"Got any good whiskey?"

"Ain't had good whiskey in the dozen years I've run the place. No un's gone blind from this batch. That's as good as whiskey gets in this saloon."

"Hello, May."

A smile flashed over her tired face. "Knew you'd be back, Kepler. You look plum full of lonesome."

"June." The name stuck in my throat.

"I know." Tears filled May's eyes. "I heard the devil took our little girl."

"I need to tell you how it happened. And about our . . ." My voice failed.

"Baby? She wrote me a letter to tell me." May splashed whiskey into two glasses. She slid one across the bar and pulled the other close to her. "June would have been a good mother. Remember how she carried on about that old cat of hers?" Her tears watered her whiskey. "Too much bad in this world. That's why June got took away. Put no blame on yourself, Kepler."

Her words touched the emptiness that lived inside of me. I drained my glass and tapped it on the bar, wanting more of May's bad whiskey to fill the hole in my soul.

She shook her head. Perhaps, May had served too many lonely, desperate men before me. She took a bundle from beneath the bar, tilted her head toward an empty table, and motioned for me to follow. I snatched up the bottle and went with her.

"A drummer left this with one of my girls just a couple weeks ago." She spread a sheet of newsprint on the table. "It's all about that circus that Bill Cody's plannin'."

"So the rumors are true," I said as I scanned the paper. Certain there was an appetite for the adventures glorified in dime novels, Cody had begun to spread stories of a grand Wild West Show that would perform in the cities of the East and then tour the world. He had promised unimaginable fame and wealth to those who would join him. "But why save this for me?"

"The fella that left this was here lookin' for cowhands, trappers, and such that would want to join in the child's play. Sheriff Beard sold him some of his horses."

"I was planning on seeing my old friend while I'm here."

"You best hurry then. Beard and that old Indian, Joe Medicine Pony, left at first light day before yesterday. They're herding those horses east to meet up with Cody's circus."

"Must be worth his while to travel that far."

"It's not the money Beard's after. It was what he saw on that paper there." May pointed to a picture at the lower corner.

Surrounded by images of stampeding buffalo, runaway stagecoaches, and Indian war dances, I squinted to where May pointed and then jerked my head up to stare at her. My hand reached for the whiskey bottle. May slapped it away.

I read the words on the page again:

Prairie Wolves: The scourge of the Plains

These viscous beasts can only be tamed by the whip and courage of this beautiful woman.

The woman in the grainy image on the paper was Landry. I had no doubt.

"You know the place where Cody's havin' 'em meet up, Kepler?"

Every fiber in me trembled. Not with fear. This would not be a crusade to stop evil. I wanted revenge.

"I do. It's an island on the Platte River in Western Nebraska. The locals call the place Reproach." This time I poured the whiskey. "My mother owns that island."

Acknowledgments

It's not so much that stories come from a deep spot in the imagination of an author. They might begin there. I believe stories in books come to life from the critique, correction, help, and encouragement of others. At least, that happened for this writer.

Thank you to the critique group that boosted my confidence in the words I wrote. Mary Ann, Liesa, ZJ, Mindy, Janet, Lizzie, Sue, Mike, Robin, Jess, Kathy, Ed—each one of you contributed.

Rocky Mountain Fiction Writers taught me the craft and business of becoming an author.

Appreciation goes to my agent, Gina Panettieri, who found a home for this manuscript, guided me through the process, and continues to believe in this storyteller.

To my editor, Carlisa Cramer, who helped me make this story better, thanks for all your help.

To Mari Kesselring and the team at North Star Editions, thank you for introducing Kepler to my readers.

And to my proofreader, partner, and wife, Nancy, all my love.

About the Author

Kevin Wolf's debut novel, *The Homeplace*, is the winner of the 2015 Tony Hillerman Award. The great-grandson of Colorado homesteaders, Wolf enjoys fly-fishing, old Winchesteres, 1950s Western movies, and the occasional bump in the night. He lives in Littleton, Colorado, with his wife and two beagles.

Previously Published

The Homeplace: St. Martin's Press (Minotaur), September 2016
Brokeheart: North Star Editions, October 2016